# CATCHING FOREVER

## *by*

## *Laurel Dee Gugler*

OUR LADY OF MT. CARMEL SCHOOL
6525 Carlton Avenue
Niagara Falls, Ontario  **L2G 5K4**

James Lorimer & Company Ltd., Publishers
Toronto

James Lorimer & Company Ltd. acknowledges the support of the Ontario Arts Council. We acknowledge the support of the Government of Canada through the Book Publishing Industry Development Program (BPIDP) for our publishing activities. We acknowledge the support of the Canada Council for the Arts for our publishing program. We acknowledge the support of the Government of Ontario through the Ontario Media Development Corporation's Ontario Book Initiative.

Series cover design: Iris Glaser

The Canada Council | Le Conseil des Arts
for the Arts | du Canada

ONTARIO ARTS COUNCIL
CONSEIL DES ARTS DE L'ONTARIO

**Library and Archives Canada Cataloguing in Publication**

Gugler, Laurel Dee
    Catching forever / Laurel Dee Gugler.

ISBN-13: 978-1-55028-954-1

    1. Mennonites — Juvenile fiction. I. Title.

| PS8567.U44C38 2007 | jC813'.54 | C2007-900351-6 |

James Lorimer & Company Ltd.,
Publishers
317 Adelaide Street West
Suite 1002
Toronto, Ontario, M5V 1P9
www.lorimer.ca
Printed and bound in Canada.

Distributed in the
United States by:
Orca Book Publishers
P.O. Box 468
Custer, WA USA
98240-0468

*To the memory of my daughter,*
*Dawn — a well-loved piece of forever*
*L.D.G.*

# 1

## If I was Spunky

I rest in the branches of Grandmother Oak, my thinking tree. A breeze tickles my neck and plays with my hair. The leaves swish and whisper. My special place has a comfortable spot to sit, almost like someone's lap. Branches reach around like arms. I come to Grandmother Oak when I need to figure something out. Or if I just want to be alone. Today I brought *Anne of Green Gables*. Mostly though, instead of reading, I'm just thinking about stuff.

Our teacher last year said Anne of Green Gables was spunky. Wish I was spunky. Grandmother Oak sighs. Or was that me? If I was spunky, I'd laugh, sing in a big voice — maybe even dance. Most people at our church, a Mennonite church, think it's a sin to dance, or at least an almost-sin. Except for my Aunt Bette. She loves to dance. If I was spunky, I'd have lots of friends. I'd know just what to say to other kids, instead of thinking later about what I wish I'd said.

*And* I would have known what to say to that snooty kid, Judy, at that horrible camp this summer. Mamma made me go because it was a Christian camp. She wants me to learn more Bible stuff. Well, Christian camp or not, that Judy girl was *mean*. She wouldn't stop picking on me for wearing dresses at camp. I can't help it if Mamma won't let me wear jeans.

"How come you dress like an old lady, Rose?" Judy said.

"How come you can't even swim?"

"How come you're by yourself all the time?"

On and on. Blah, blah, blah!

The only good thing about camp was the singing. I especially liked the silly Noah song.

*God said to Noah, There's gonna be a floody, floody*
*Get those children out of the muddy, muddy,*

*Children of the Lord*

There are about a gazillion goofy verses.

I'm afraid this week will be just as bad as that week at camp. I have to go to a new school tomorrow — Prairie View Elementary. My old school, Lone Tree, closed down. And to make it a thousand times worse, Judy goes to Prairie View. If I was spunky I wouldn't even mind. If she picked on me, maybe I'd just bash her over the head like Anne did to Gilbert Blythe. Ha! Wouldn't she be surprised. 'Course, Mennonites aren't supposed to do stuff like that. We're supposed to be peaceful every single minute and never ever fight. *Why was I born Mennonite?* One of those why-of-things questions. I wonder about the why of things when I'm with Grandmother Oak. Why was I born here on a small American farm where there is plenty to eat, and some other kid was born in Africa and is starving? Why was I born a girl and not a boy? Or why was I born at all? And why am I living now, in 1955, instead of a hundred years ago, or a hundred years from now? I wonder stuff like that. I wonder if other kids think about such things.

I don't have a real grandmother — not anymore. One of my grandmothers died long before I was born. My other grandmother died when I was two years old. I can just barely remember her wrinkly, crinkly face and twinkly gray eyes. I used to sit on her lap and she'd read me Bible stories or farm magazines. Mamma says I'd toddle to her with a book and say, "Rose looky booky." Sounds *embarrassing* now. I'll bet Grandmother wondered about the why of things too. Otherwise, why would she have read to me? Or could it be that she just liked holding me?

I don't remember sitting on Mamma's or Papa's lap. They aren't the hug-and-snuggle type. Mamma is like Marilla in *Anne of Green Gables*. She thinks imagining things is *Dummheit*. That's a German word that means silliness. Papa is quieter than Mamma, sort of like Marilla's brother, Matthew, though not quite as shy. He understands me better than Mamma does, though I would *never* think of talking to him like I talk to Grandmother Oak.

From high in the tree, I see cornfields, plowed wheat fields, and the pasture where cows are grazing. So flat, I almost feel like I can see into forever. When I squint, sometimes I catch a glimpse of a shimmery forever-place between where the ground and sky come together.

Up close I see Daniel and our cat Stinker in the vegetable garden beside our house. Daniel is hunched on the ground, looking at something. Probably some worm or bug. He loves creepy-crawly critters. Stinker pokes at whatever it is with her paw. We named her Stinker because she got sprayed by a skunk when she was little. Poor kitty! Anyway, I love my little brother. Sometimes I have the same feeling about Daniel that I did when Stinker got too close to the cows, when she was a kitten, and I worried that she'd get trampled. Daniel looks a little … different. He is four years old and small for his age. He squints through big, dark-rimmed glasses and is cross-eyed. He has a wide gap between his front teeth. And he can't say his l's. He says "wadybug" instead of ladybug, and "bumbo bee" instead of bumble bee. I'm glad he doesn't start school this year. Kids might pick on him. If only *I* didn't have to go to school.

# 2

## Not Chosen

The first day at our new school, Prairie View, butterflies flitter-flutter in my belly. Actually it's more like jackrabbits jumping about in there.

"I wish this day was over," I say to my friend, Sandra, as we walk along the gravelly road to school. "I wish the whole year was over." Sandra is my only friend. She's even shyer than I am.

She doesn't answer. Just walks along, real stiff-like. I kick bits of gravel ahead of me.

"You'll scuff your shoes."

"Mercy sakes, you sound like Mamma." Everything about Sandra is tidy — her long, brown hair, her socks that never sag, her polished shoes. How can she keep her shoes shiny on a dusty road? Her dress, though, like mine, is too long.

"There's this snooty kid who was at camp," I tell Sandra, "who goes to Prairie View — Snooty Judy."

"You shouldn't call her that, Rose."

"Well, she *is* snooty. She was horribly mean to me at camp — laughed at my dresses, bossed me around. I wish we could keep going to Lone Tree." I like the name Lone Tree. It reminds me of Grandmother Oak, though I don't say this to Sandra. I don't know why it was called Lone Tree. There wasn't even one single tree on the schoolyard.

"There weren't enough kids at Lone Tree to keep it open," says Sandra.

"I *know*, I *know!* But don't you ever feel like grumbling?"

"It's not nice."

*Achhh!* I wish Sandra would be more of a gripe-and-grumble friend, and not so perfect. But I guess she doesn't do as many sins as I do. Talking about Snooty Judy the way I do is a gossipy sort of sin.

The closer we get to school, the slower I walk.

"We'll be late," says Sandra.

"No we won't." I keep poking along. I want to get there just exactly in time for the bell. I don't want to talk to the other kids, or give them time to tease me. Probably the other girls will be wearing jeans. Mamma doesn't believe in girls wearing jeans. Not ladylike, she says. Who wants to be ladylike anyway? Shucks! Mamma sews my dresses. She makes them too long — wants me to be modest.

As we walk into the schoolyard, my belly feels jumpier than ever. My throat is dry. And just as I thought, all the other girls are wearing jeans. And there is Judy with her nose in the air, looking as snooty as ever.

"Look at these two old ladies," she hoots. She comes over and pulls at Sandra's dress. Then mine. "Your mamma didn't make them long *enough*," she taunts. "We still see your legs." My face gets as hot as our basement furnace.

The bell rings. Thank goodness!

We go inside. Straight rows of wooden desks. The smell of chalk and wood. Sandra and I find desks near each other. The only kids I know are the Lone Tree kids. Our teacher, Mr. Ford, says, "We are happy to have boys and girls from Lone Tree join us this year. I'm sure the rest of you will make them feel welcome."

I glance at Snooty Judy, who rolls her eyes. She sees my glance and sticks out her tongue. My furnace face burns. We get to work. Math and reading. Good! Numbers and words and things I can figure out. Wish I could figure out what to do around snooty kids. Recess comes too soon. Sandra and I walk outside together.

"Here comes the two old ladies," snorts Snooty Judy.

I hate this, hate this, hate this! There must be an easier way to learn stuff than coming to school.

"Let's play ball," yells someone.

"Yeah, we'll chose sides."

We didn't play softball at Lone Tree.

We played hide-and-seek in the neighbour's cornfield. Put planks across the ditches to make hideouts — one for the girls and one for the boys. Picked daisies in the schoolyard meadow. Hunted for treasures — marbles, buttons, coloured glass, meadowlark feathers, stuff like that.

But there's no use thinking about these things. Tom and Snooty Judy are already choosing sides. They choose their friends. Soon only the Lone Tree kids are left. Then only Norman, Fred, Sandra and me.

Snooty Judy scowls. "Looks like a bunch of losers." Then sighs. "Norman."

"Fred," calls Tom.

Only Sandra and me are left. The back of my eyes sting.

Jabbing an angry finger in my direction, Snooty Judy says, "I'll take what's-her-name." She *knows* my name is Rose.

Then Sandra, last of all. At least I'm not quite last, though I feel bad thinking this. I see Sandra gulp down tears. I put my hand on her shoulder, but she gets all stiff. I quickly take off my hand.

The game begins, and I want recess to be over. The other team is up to bat first. I go way out into left field. Surely a ball won't come this far. No such luck! Tom hits the ball which rolls in my direction. Oh help! I cup my hands awkwardly to the ground. The ball rolls between my legs.

"Loser!" yells Snooty Judy.

Everyone on our team moans. I swallow tears as I turn to get the ball. Tom gets to third base. I throw the ball weakly towards the catcher. It gets only halfway. The taunts get louder.

"A Lone Tree loser. We don't want any Lone Tree losers on our side."

"No wonder you can't play in that old-lady dress," says Snooty Judy.

When our team goes to bat, I go to the end of the line. Surely recess will be over before it's my turn. I don't pay attention to what's happening in the game. I only watch the batting line, and listen for the bell. But recess seems to go on forever. The batting line gets shorter until there's only one person ahead of me.

*R-r-r-ring!*

Saved! Love that bell.

But lunch and afternoon recess are just as bad — softball again. Is that all they ever play? All I want to do is go home.

# 3

## Smad

When I get home, Daniel comes running, a big grin on his face.

"Leave me alone!" My angry words burst out. Daniel's eyes open wide in hurt surprise. His lips tremble. I'm sorry right away, *but I just have to get away*. I run from him.

Beside the barn, I pick up a short, fat piece of branch lying under Grandmother Oak. I whack the side of the barn.

Who do all those dumb kids think they are? *Bam!*

Who does Snooty Judy think she is, the king of the world? *Bam!*

Somebody ought to teach her a lesson. *Bam!*

Then I start to cry. I climb into the arms of Grandmother Oak. She whispers in a friendly way while I sob ... and sob. *I'm so mad!* And sad. *Smad,* I think — half mad, and half sad. I say it out loud, "smad." A good word. My Sunday school teacher says we're supposed to love our enemies. Sorry God, I just can't do it.

*Why are some people nice and others so nasty?* "Hmm, guess we won't figure that out today, Grandmother Oak. And what should I do about school?"

I imagine Grandmother's voice. *So you weren't good at softball. So what? You never had any practice. But you can learn, and be just as good as any of those kids.*

"Yeah, I need a ball, a bat, and a glove. How will I get them? No use asking Mamma. She'll think it's *Dummheit*. No use trying to earn money. We have lots of chores, but we sure don't get paid." I sigh and close my eyes.

Aunt Bette! That's it! She might have softball stuff that isn't being used anymore. Her daughter, my cousin Fran is grown up and has moved away. I'll ask Aunt Bette about softball stuff in church next Sunday. Yeah! I feel better with a plan.

Aunt Bette is Mamma's sister but they're sure not alike. Mamma thinks Aunt Bette's ways are *Dummheit*. Aunt Bette has a huge purple hat, and lots of other big hats. People call her Big Hat Bette. She wears long skirts with big flowers. And she wears jingly bracelets and long jangly earrings. Most women in our church don't wear earrings. Some people at our church think jewellery is a sin — especially the big, dangle-jangle kind. But Aunt Bette doesn't care. She just jingles her way merrily along. And she does other things that folks around here don't do, like going to the theatre. Theatre is another almost-sin around here. Oh, and she has paintings of naked people. I think that's a for-sure sin. And she is a huggy sort of person, and she has a big bosom that I sink into when she hugs me. I giggle, thinking of this. People say she is eccentric. I think I'll be eccentric when I grow up.

When I come down from Grandmother Oak, I pick up the same big branch I had before. I find a good stone, toss it in the air, and swing the branch-bat. I miss. I try a few more times. Mostly, I miss.

Finally I shuffle towards the house, kicking the stone ahead of me as I go. Daniel is playing in front of the house. He zooms back and forth making tractor sounds.

"Putt-putt-putt. Putt-putt-putt. Putt-putt-putt."

He sees me and quickly looks away.

"Daniel," I call.

The tractor gets louder. "Putt-putt-putt! Putt-putt-putt! Putt-putt-putt!"

I chase the tractor as it zooms this way and that. "I'm sorry I shouted at you."

"You're mean!" yells the tractor, in between putt-putts.

Finally the putt-putting stops long enough for me to say, "I'm sorry, Daniel." I face him and put my hands on his shoulders. He tries to wiggle away, but I hold tight, one hand on each shoulder. Again I say, "Daniel, I'm sorry I yelled when I came home. I was … I was … smad." I decide to share the word.

"S-smad?" He looks at me and squishes up his face.

"Yeah. It means partly mad and partly sad."

Daniel thinks about this, then asks, "Were you smad at *me*?"

"No, Daniel." I hug him and he doesn't pull away. "I wasn't smad at you. I was smad at some kids at school. They were nasty to me."

"Oh." He puts his hand into mine and looks up into my face, his eyes big with worry.

"Come on," I say, "I'll teach you a silly song. *God said to Noah, there's gonna be a floody, floody … Get those children out of the muddy, muddy …*"

He giggles and sings after me, *"God said to Noah, there's gonna be a fwoody, fwoody … Get those chiwdren out of the muddy, muddy …"*

He sings the whole crazy song after me, and fills it with his jingly little laugh — sprinkles of sound on the air.

> *God said to Noah, there's gonna be a floody, floody*
> *God said to Noah, there's gonna be a floody, floody*
> *Get those children out of the muddy, muddy*
> *Children of the Lord.*

*God said to Noah, you better build an arky,*
*arky*
*God said to Noah, you better build an arky,*
*arky*
*Build it out of hickory barky, barky*
*Children of the Lord.*
*The animals, they came on board by twosies,*
*twosies, twosies*
*Animals, they came on board by twosies,*
*twosies, twosies*
*Elephants and kangaroosies, roosies*
*Children of the Lord.*
*It rained and poured for forty daysies,*
*daysies*
*Rained and poured for forty daysies, daysies*
*Nearly drove those animals crazies, crazies*
*Children of the Lord.*
*The sun came out and dried up all the*
*landy, landy, landy*
*Sun came out and dried up all the landy,*
*landy, landy*
*Everything was fine and dandy, dandy*
*Children of the Lord.*

# 4

## A Moment Caught Forever

Finally, it's Friday. No more softball till Monday. I thought this week would last forever.

Mamma pokes her head out the door when I turn into the driveway after school. "Pick up the mail, Rose," she calls.

I yank open the door of our metal mailbox at the end of the driveway. Only two things — a newspaper called *The Farm Journal* and a letter. It's for *me!* I have *never* gotten mail before. I thought only important people got letters. A square envelope with my name neatly written — Rose Penner. The return address says Mary Schmidt. She was my camp counsellor. The thought of that awful week makes me feel smad, smad, smad! And ashamed. My cheeks burn when I think about Snooty Judy and some of the others teasing me about my dresses. *Imagine!* Wearing dresses at camp. Anyway, *I can't believe I got a letter!* I open it quickly. It is a photo of a smiling girl singing. *Can that be me?* I get only the tiniest glance, because Mamma is at the door again. I slip the photo and envelope into my pocket. I hope she didn't see.

"What's in the mail?" she calls.

*"The Farm Journal."* I don't tell her about my letter. I dash into the house and plunk the news-paper on the table in front of Mamma. She is stringing a huge mountain of green beans. I start to run to Grandmother Oak to have a close look at the photo. No such luck.

"Help me string these beans, Rose."

I sigh, sit, and string. Mamma does look tired. Her face kind of sags. So does the apron that hangs over her shoulder. I have the jittery-twitters. I keep reaching under the table to pat my pocket and feel the flat photo. My feet tap-tap on the floor.

"Stop fidgeting," says Mamma. "How was

school today?" She pushes her sagging apron strap back over her shoulder. I don't think she really wants to know. Her eyes are looking inside her own head, her mind someplace else. Well, that makes two of us.

"Fine," Uh-oh! I just did another sin. That lie slipped out so quickly.

I don't tell Mamma that I struck out at softball. I don't tell her that my stupid dress got in my way when we played ball. I don't tell her that Snooty Judy called me Lone Tree Loser.

Mamma isn't a tell-your-troubles-to sort of Mamma. If I do try to tell her things, she just gets upset. Then I feel smadder than ever.

The green-bean mountain gets *slowly* smaller. Finally, we're finished. I dash out the kitchen door.

"Not so fast," Mamma yells after me. "Time to gather the eggs."

*Achhh!* My insides scream. Mamma always gives me a gazillion chores. Go weed the garden. Go feed the pigs. Go do this. Go do that.

On the way to the henhouse, I start to take out the photo, but *oh no*, here comes Daniel, happily singing. *"God said to Noah, You better biwd an arky, arky...."*

Quickly I push the photo back into my pocket. Daniel is holding a beetle. He's forever catching bugs and stuff. "Wook, Rose, I catched it. Did two beed-os go on the arky, arky?"

"Yes," I say. "A man beetle and a woman beetle went onto the arky, arky." We both laugh. "Daniel, I gotta go...."

But sometimes it's as hard to get away from him as from Mamma's chores.

"Oh *wook*, Rose." A ladybug just landed on his arm. He laughs. "Did two wadybugs go on the arky, arky?"

"Uh-huh. Two wady ... I mean ladybugs." All I want to do is look at my photo, and here I am talking about wadybugs and arky, arkys."

"A man wadybug and a woman wadybug?"

"Uh-huh. I gotta go gather the eggs, Daniel." I start to run, but he calls after me.

"But Rose, how can there be a *man* wadybug?"

"They're just called that," I shout back. "It doesn't mean all ladybugs are girl bugs."

"Did two spiders …"

But I'm already in the henhouse. "Oh Yeck!" I step on a big blob of chicken manure, and for just a minute, I wish two chickens hadn't gone onto the ark.

I don't even try to look at my mail until I'm finished with chores and no one is around to bother me.

Finally, I climb onto Grandmother Oak's lap. I put green-bean mountains, beed-os, wadybugs, and arky, arkys right out of my head. Even Snooty Judy. No room for her in my head right now. "Hello Grandmother. I got some mail." I settle into my cosy place. Now that I'm *finally* here, somehow I don't want to look quite yet. Strange. Again I touch my pocket. Then ever so slowly, I take out the envelope and slip out the photo. I still don't look — just hold it between my palms. I feel flitter-fluttery. The leaves tremble.

"Is the girl in the photo really me, Grandmother?"

She whispers in a lullaby voice.

I look.

The girl in the photo has sparkling eyes and

her mouth is open wide. She's … yes … beautiful. And it's me. *It's really me.* The embarrassing dress is barely noticeable. All I can see is the shining face singing.

Carefully I put the photo back into the envelope. Oh! There are words on the back.

"To Rose — a moment in your life, caught forever."

# 5

## Smurt

Today I'm happy to go to church because I'm going to ask Aunt Bette whether she has softball stuff. I hope! I hope! I hope! Besides, it's better than going to school and being around Judy.

It's getting late and Papa is still wearing overalls and Daniel is wearing only underwear.

"Hurry and get dressed," says Mamma.

She's already dressed in a sky-blue dress with tiny purple flowers. It's her one store-bought dress. She looks nice. The blue looks good with her grey-and-black hair. She rolls her hair in a circle around the top of her head.

"I'll bet God wouldn't mind if I went to church in overalls," says Papa. He smiles at me.

"What do you think, my Rose?"

My Rose. I love it when he says that.

"I'm sure he wouldn't mind," I say. Papa hates wearing a suit. He's happiest in his overalls and John Deere farm hat.

"Would God mind if I went to church in my underwear?" asks Daniel.

We laugh. Even Mamma smiles.

"Well, my boy," says Papa, "God brought you into this world with less than your underwear, so how could he object?"

"Don't be ridiculous," says Mamma, no longer smiling.

Papa puts on his suit, and Daniel puts on his best shirt and pants.

***

We have a big church. About six hundred people. First there's the church service, then Sunday school.

We're almost late, but I'm glad because the only place there's still room is the balcony — my favourite place. Daniel and I sit between Mamma and Papa. I fold a handkerchief in a special way to make a pretend mouse. I give it to Daniel. It helps keep him quiet.

I've figured out some balcony games to make time go faster during long, boring sermons. I look down and count bald heads, or look at the women's hats. Most of the hats are dark, except for Aunt Bette's. Sometimes I make up *what would happen if* games.

What would happen if I walked along the balcony railing? Would the preacher yell at me? Or would he go right on preaching? What would happen if I dropped my Sunday school book over the edge of the balcony? What would happen if I used someone's bald head for target practice? Maybe I could aim my Sunday school quarter at one of those shiny heads.

Once, I told Sandra about the *what would happen if* game, but she frowned — wasn't interested. She doesn't do silly things. Maybe she's afraid to even think funny thoughts. Our preacher says God knows our thoughts. If God punished people for thinking silly thoughts, I'd be in *big* trouble.

Today, along with these balcony games, I look for Aunt Bette. Doesn't take long. She's wearing a big purple hat and a purple shawl. I can't wait for church and Sunday school to be over so I can ask her about the softball stuff. And all the while, I half-listen to the preacher. He is talking about this Nicodemus guy who wants to become a whole new person. I think about my camp photo. I look like a whole new person in that photo. Anyway, Nicodemus goes to Jesus for help. I wonder if there were Snooty Judy type people bothering Nicodemus. Oh! I think the preacher said Nicodemus was a *Pharisee* and too proud. He was one of the snooty types himself. But he wasn't happy. I wonder if Snooty Judy is happy. Hmmm! Judy! She's the biggest thought in my head these days. What would a whole new person do about Judy? *Love your enemies.* Inside my head I say, *I love you Judy.* But that's a lie. I either do a sin by lying, or do a sin by hating her. Since it's a sin either way, I may as well keep on hating her. I'm sure not a whole new person yet. I sigh. Oops, kinda loud. Mamma puts her hand firmly on my knee. That means behave. It's hard to sit still, though. Daniel makes it even harder by making his hanky-mouse creep across my lap. What would happen if I yelled, "Eeek, there's a mouse in my lap."

\*\*\*

When church and Sunday school are finally over, I wind my way through the crowd looking for Aunt Bette. I keep my eyes peeled for purple. At last I see her hat bobbing along in the crowd. I chase the hat, winding in and out until I'm beside her.

"Hi, Aunt Bette."

"Well, hi there, luv. How's my favourite niece?" I'm her only niece, but I like the way she says that anyway. She hugs me and I sink into her softness.

"Do you have softball stuff I can use?" I ask. "A bat, ball, and a glove? I need to practise for school."

"As a matter of fact, an old bat fell off the closet shelf just the other day. Fell on my toe. I cursed a bit." She leans towards my ear and whispers,

"Don't tell the preacher." I nod and laugh. "And I'm sure I have a ball too. As for a glove, I'm afraid you're on your own."

"Oh, oh, oh! I can start practising." I get up and do a little dance. I'm so excited, I hardly care about the glove. I do one more twirl, but then see a sour-faced man glaring at me. "Aunt Bette, is it a sin to dance?"

"Oh, sweetheart, this old gal thinks it's a sin *not* to dance. Folks need a way to show happiness. "

My eyes open wide. I giggle.

"That's the spirit," she says. "And it's a sin not to laugh."

My giggle bursts bigger. "Yeah," I add, "and it's a big sin not to sing."

"Absolutely," says Aunt Bette.

"*You put your right foot in. You take your right foot out.*" I quietly start to sing a song we learned at camp. But Aunt Bette belts it out, not quietly at all. "*You do the hokey-pokey and you turn yourself around. That's what it's all about.*"

A little boy comes hokey-pokeying over, wide-eyed, and smiling, but his stern-faced mamma pulls him away. "Really," she says. "Such carrying on, and in a *church!*"

When the song is finished, Aunt Bette says, "Darlin', the real sin is when we don't use our God-given talents to express who we are."

Aunt Bette lots of times talks to me in grown-up ways. I like that. Usually, I understand her, though sometimes it takes some puzzling out.

"Now," she asks, "How is your new school going?"

I don't feel like dancing anymore. I look down.

"That bad, huh? Come sit a minute," she says, taking my hand. She leads me to a pew, her flowered skirt flowing. "Now, tell me about it."

"I hate it!" Rather than look at her face, I stare at a big purple flower in her skirt. "I'm no good at softball. We never played it at Lone Tree. And the kids are so snobby, and I hate wearing dresses when the other girls wear jeans." I hadn't meant to say all that.

She nods and puts her hand on my shoulder. Suddenly I feel like crying. But I won't. Not here. But I do tell her more stuff, about how the other kids are mean to the Lone Tree kids, how they call us Lone Tree losers. I even tell her my word, smad.

Again she nods, thinks for a while.

"Smurt!" she says, finally.

"Smurt?"

"I think maybe you feel smurt — partly smad, partly hurt. It hurts when others don't treat you right."

"Yeah." The word makes me feel like laughing and crying at the same time. But I don't want to talk about it anymore. "I gotta go now."

"Okay, luv. Good thinking to ask about softball equipment. With practice, you'll be as good as the rest of them in no time. After all, you have a natural ability."

"I do?" I'm amazed.

"Of course! I've seen you swinging in a tree like a monkey. You have ability in physical activities, and I have a hunch that includes all kinds of sports. I'll bring the ball and bat over tomorrow, when I pick up some string beans your mamma said she has for me."

She hugs me again, then goes, her long skirt swish-swishing.

# 6

## Cahoots

"Old lady number one," says Judy, tugging on Sandra's dress, "and old lady number two." She tugs on mine. Then she goes back to Sandra. Judy is even nastier to Sandra than she is to me. "Stinky Sandra's stinky sandwich," she chants as we sit in the schoolyard having lunch. She dances around Sandra, who sort of shrinks. Judy puffs herself up like a mean old rooster. Sandra's cheese sandwich is pretty smelly alright, but Judy makes it sound like Sandra is stinky, too. I don't know why Sandra keeps bringing those stupid sandwiches. When Sandra finishes her sandwich, she takes a chocolate cupcake from her lunchbox. It has pink frosting and even a red cherry on top.

A tiny smile curls the corners of her mouth.

"Well for once you have something good," says Judy. "Something besides those barfy cheese sandwiches. You don't deserve anything good." She grabs the cupcake, then makes a big show of eating it. Still prancing around Sandra, she smacks her lips. "Don't you wish *you* had a cupcake? It's so-o-o good!" Sandra just sits there, hunched and red-faced. And me — I just sit there, too. I should say something. But if I do, Judy will start in on me. I feel bad for not speaking up. What would a spunky kid do?

The only thing that cheers me is that I now have Aunt Bette's ball and bat. I'll practise tonight.

After school I run to the barn to find Papa. "Papa, Papa, will you practise ball with me?"

"After supper and dishwashing, my Rose."

His words feel warm in my belly. "Oh thank you, Papa!"

Papa is milking Dancer. We named her Dancer because she used to kick a lot, dancing and prancing, when Papa tried to milk her. Sometimes she put her foot right into the milk pail. But Papa gentled her.

Papa sits hunched on a wooden milk stool at Dancer's side. The frothing milk streams into the pail.

Zum-zum! Zum-zum!

Daniel and I call cows' udders "zum-zums" because of the sound of milk streaming into the pail.

Papa talks softly to Dancer as he milks. "Steady there, Dancer."

He looks up and smiles at me just as she switches her tail, whacking Papa across the face. Oooh, I know how that stings. It has happened to me when I've helped with the milking. Dancer isn't being mean. She switches her tail to keep the flies off.

Papa turns back to Dancer's side, protecting his face.

As Papa keeps zum-zumming, I hurry away to do the chicken chores.

I change my clothes, grab the wire basket to gather eggs, and dash out to the hen house. I have to step carefully around little blobs of fresh, squishy, icky chicken manure. In the summer, when I'm barefoot, manure squishes between my toes if I don't step carefully. *Yech!* Rows of wooden nests line the walls of the henhouse. Though the hens are meant to lay their eggs in these nests, they don't always follow the rules. Often they lay their eggs any old place, some-times not even in the henhouse.

"Good for you," I say as I pick up an egg from the middle of the floor. "You lay your eggs wher-ever you please."

I'm beginning to think like Aunt Bette. Laying eggs any old place reminds me of colouring out-side the lines. Aunt Bette doesn't believe in colouring books where you have to colour inside the lines.

One cross old hen — one of the rule-followers — sits on her eggs in a nest, making angry cluck-ing noises. I reach under her for the eggs.

Peck, peck, peck!

"Ouch!" Her sharp beak peppers my hand. Can't blame her really.

I find a stick and gently hold her head down so she can't peck, then reach underneath for the eggs. "Sorry," I say, "I know you're just protecting your eggs, but I have to gather them."

After supper Mamma shells peas at the kitchen table and Papa dozes on the corner couch. *Oh dear, he said he'd practise with me.* I wash dishes without dawdling or complaining. Daniel, standing on a chair beside me, helps rinse. But mostly he splish-splashes about. He holds up a strainer and lets the water sprinkle through it.

"Wook, Rose," he says, "I can make it rain."

"We can use you to water the fields," says Papa, his eyes still closed. "I could sure use a rainmaker."

Oh good! Papa isn't asleep after all.

Daniel giggles, still happily splashing about. "I'm a rainmaker."

"Stop splish-splashing," I say. "You made my dress wet."

"I *wike* spwish-spwashing."

When we're finally finished, I ask, "Papa, can we practise ball now?"

"Oh, *that's* why you're being so quick and helpful," says Mamma. "What about your homework?"

"I think ball practise *is* her homework," says Papa. He smiles at me. This minute I love him to bits.

Throwing up her hands, Mamma says, "You two are in cahoots."

"Ca-*hooots!*" crows Daniel gleefully.

"Cahoots," says Papa. "It means collusion." He likes showing off his big words.

"Co-*woo*-sion," shouts Daniel. His eyes twinkle and his mouth makes a big "O" at the "woo" sound.

"For heaven's sake," says Mamma, "he's only four years old.

"Doesn't mean he can't learn new words," says Papa. "Cahoots. Collusion. Means planning something together — sometimes with a hint of mirth."

"Hinto-mirth," sings Daniel.

I burst out laughing.

"Hint of mirth, indeed," mumbles Mamma.

Papa and I go out to practise, though I can see he's tired. To show him how I feel, I take his hand, though I'm too big for such stuff. He looks surprised, but I know he's pleased. He roughs my hair like he did when I was little.

"Papa, could you pitch please? I need batting practice."

"Okay, we'll have you hitting home runs in no time."

Papa does a strange windmill thing, spinning his arms around and around. He doesn't look tired anymore.

"What are you *doing*, Papa?" I try not to laugh.

"This is the windup."

Well, in his windup, the ball slips out of his hand and rolls uselessly. I giggle.

"Laughing at your poor old Papa, are you?" He winks at me. "Okay, no more fancy stuff. Nice and easy."

His nice-and-easy pitch falls to the ground before it gets to me.

"Oops! Just got to get the hang of it."

But all of his pitches are awful. They're too high, too low, or way to the side. Finally, I start swinging at nearly all of his pitches because there is no point waiting for a good one.

"I'm afraid I'm not very good at this," he says. He looks tired again. Stinker is having fun, though, chasing the ball when it rolls on the ground.

"It's okay. Maybe you can throw the ball so I can practise catching."

Well, he doesn't have a natural ability at that, either.

I have one more idea. "Could you roll me some really fast balls? I need practise in scooping up ground balls. Sometimes they roll right through my legs."

"Well, I think even I can manage that."

Mostly, though, I know I'll get very little help from him.

Over the next few days, I figure out ways to practise by myself. I throw the ball as high as I can, then catch it when it comes down. Sometimes I throw it up and a bit to the side, so I have to run and figure out where it will come down. And sometimes I bounce Daniel's rubber ball against the garage wall, then catch it when it bounces back. Of course, catching a rubber ball isn't the same as catching a softball, but it's better than not practising at all. By springtime I'm gonna be as good as the rest of them.

# 7

# Flunked Spunk

Aunt Bette and I sit under Grandmother Oak. I'm feeling as unspunky as unspunky can be. I'm thinking how I didn't know what to say to Judy when she bugged us about our dresses — and Sandra about her sandwich. I sort of want to talk about school stuff. But right now I can't bring myself to do it — not even with Aunt Bette. I'm afraid I might start crying or something. I stir around in the dirt with a stick.

"Is something on your mind?" asks Aunt Bette.

"Nah." I sigh. Another lie.

"You know, when I was your age, I didn't like school much," says Aunt Bette.

"You *didn't*? Why not?"

"Couldn't sit still. Couldn't keep my mouth shut. Even got the strap from time to time."

"*Really?* What did you do to get the strap?"

"Once, when the teacher was out of the room, I stood on my desk and did a little wiggle-hip jig."

I laugh.

"The teacher came back and caught me. Marched me in front of the whole class, and strapped the palms of my hands."

"Did you cry?"

"My eyes filled with tears. But I didn't make a sound."

"I remember my first day at Lone Tree," I tell her. "I couldn't sit still, either."

"What happened?"

"I sat at a wooden desk, all wiggly, legs swinging, waiting for fun stuff to happen."

"Ahhh!" hoots Aunt Bette. "You have to wait a *looong* time for the fun to begin in these stodgy old schools."

"Finally, I couldn't stand it *any* longer. I got up and ran around and around the schoolroom, smacking my hand on each desk as I went past. *Whap! Whap! Whap!* "

Aunt Betty hoots and slaps her thighs. "Good for you!" she shouts.

"And then this great, big shape, like a shadow — it was the teacher, but I just remember a big shadow-monster grabbing me by the shoulders and marching me back to my desk. She plunked me down into my seat. Hard! She shouted, 'You may as well learn *right now*, that's *not* the way to behave in school!' After that, I was always quiet in school."

"Oh darlin', no matter what that shadow-monster said, what you did was awfully spunky! No one below the age of ninety should *ever* have to sit quietly at a desk."

I stare at her, then grin. "Spunky, huh?"

"You bet your life!"

"Well, back then, I thought, I'd done something *awful!*"

"*Awfully* spunky! You've got spunk, girl. It's just been hiding since that day. You'll figure out how to use it."

After Aunt Bette leaves, I sit thinking about what she said. *You've got spunk girl, and you'll figure out how to use it.* Maybe I'll stare Judy down when she's nasty? And for sure tell her to leave Sandra — and me — alone. I think about my camp photo. I look spunky there. I still can hardly believe it's me. I always thought I was — not pretty, not ugly, just ever so ordinary. In the photo, I look kind of sparkly, and ... even beautiful. Our preacher would say it's vain to think that, but I don't feel vain, just surprised.

At school the next day I imagine standing on my desk doing a little wiggle-hip jig, long dress and all. Wouldn't I look funny! Maybe I'd even lift my skirt just a little. I smile.

"I suggest you either share the joke or get to work," says Mr. Ford.

I pretend to get busy.

I get my first spunk test during lunch. Same old thing — Judy holds Sandra's lunch pail high above her head with one hand, and holds her nose with the other.

"Stinky Sandra's stinky sandwich!"

Though my belly wibble-wobbles, I go over to Judy and say "Leave her alone." But it comes out of my mouth sort of mumbly.

"Well now, ain't you askin' for it," says Judy. She drops the lunch pail with a mighty whang. "One old lady lookin' after the other — both Lone Tree losers."

"Leave us alone," I say, trying for a louder voice, but now my voice is wibbly-wobbly along with my belly. And I forget to look her in the eye. I just flunked spunk.

Turning away, I pick up a rubber ball from a pile of playground equipment and go to the far side of the school building — away from the other kids. Even away from Sandra. I bounce the ball off the wall. Hard! Over and over. Most of the time I catch it. I've been practising, mostly by myself, though Papa sometimes rolls ground balls for me to scoop up. Mr. Ford comes past, sees me, but doesn't say anything.

When everyone is finished lunch, it's time for our usual ball game. Today Mr. Ford comes out. Usually he stays inside during recess, I guess he does teacher stuff like marking papers. My belly tightens waiting for the awful choosing of sides. But Mr. Ford says, "Number off. The ones will be a team, and the twos another."

"Aw!" mumbles Snooty Judy, "I'll probably get stuck with lotsa Lone Tree losers." She glares at me.

Though some kids groan, others look relieved. Especially Sandra.

"And today is a good day to change positions," says Mr. Ford.

"Judy, you take right field."

"What?" she croaks.

He ignores her.

"Tom, you take left field."

Mr. Ford goes down the list, while my belly jumps and my heart thump-thumps. *I'm not ready for anything but the outfield.* But then I remember: *You've got spunk, girl!*

"Rose …"

Before Mr. Ford can finish, I say, "I'll take third base."

"Good, Rose." He smiles, but I can see the surprise in his eyes.

I didn't flunk spunk this time. Or was that just dumb? I say a small prayer inside my head. *Oh dear God, please! I don't want any balls coming this way.* The other team is up to bat first. I stand stiffly at third. Dennis, the first batter, walks. Then Cindy hits a grounder and gets to first. Dennis moves on to second. Doesn't look good. I have a bad case of the jittery-twitters, shifting from one foot to the other. Then Tom hits a grounder. My prayer is not answered. The ball is coming towards me — just to the inside of the base. I have a sick feeling. But I scoop it up! *I did it! I did it! I did it!* I touch the base. Dennis, coming from second, is out. I throw the ball to first base but it falls short. Tom makes it to first, and Cindy gets to second. Still, I feel okay. Dennis is out! *I got an out!* Whoop-de-do and hallelujah! Couldn't have done it at the beginning of the year.

But then something awful happens.

We go to bat. Batting is what worries me most, because I haven't figured out a way to practise batting by myself. When my turn comes, though, I actually hit it, and I might even have gotten to first base, except my foot somehow steps on the inside of my dress, and I stumble. I scrape my knee, but the sting on my knee is nothing compared to the stinging, burning shame I feel.

Judy chants, "I see London. I see France. I see Rose's under …"

"Enough!" thunders Mr. Ford. He comes to me, "Are you okay?"

"Yeah," says my quiet, outside voice. *No,* screams my inside voice, *I am NOT okay!* And I *hate, hate, hate* these stupid dresses that Mamma makes me wear!

When I get home, I sneak to Grandmother Oak before anyone sees me. For just a second, I think I see a wrinkled face and friendly grey eyes looking into mine. Then the face disappears, but the knobby old arms still hold me. "I gotta convince Mamma to let me have jeans," I tell her, "I just gotta!" *I see London, I see France …* I shudder with shame, remembering. Grandmother Oak trembles, too. Oh! I know what I'll say to Mamma — how it's not ladylike to wear a dress when I'm playing softball. Yeah. Tomorrow.

# 8

## The Right Time

*Mamma, it would be much more ladylike if I wore jeans for playing softball. You know, in case I fall. My dress might fly up.* I practise the words in my head.

Mamma is busy at her sewing machine. *RRRRR!* The sewing machine's rumble is almost as noisy as our tractor. Oh no! She's making me another dress — an ugly, purple paisley. How can I ask for jeans when she's sewing another dress? Maybe now isn't the right time. I grab my spelling book and sit at the table so she'll think I'm doing homework. I keep peeking up at her. She holds the straight pins in her mouth, the ends poking out. She takes them out of the dress when she doesn't need them — puts them in her mouth till she needs them again — then pokes them back into the dress. She looks tired — furrows on her forehead and dark lines under her eyes. She keeps glancing at the clock. I know she is thinking it's time to make lunch. She pins and sews, pins and sews. The sewing machine rumbles and stops, rumbles and stops.

All at once, I know I love her — lots. I don't know why I think that all of a sudden. Maybe because she looks so tired. I want to give her a kiss — just a peck on the cheek, maybe. But we don't do that at our house. Daniel and I hug each other, but that kind of happens by itself. We don't think about it or anything. I sit there thinking about giving her a kiss, but I don't. Why don't I just do it? It's not a big thing. But in our family it is. Finally, I do it — just walk over and kiss her cheek. Her eyes fly open wide. She stares at me. The pins are still in her mouth. I feel myself blushing. She takes the pins out of her mouth and turns her chair towards me.

"What was that for?" she asks.

"Because I felt like it." Somehow I can feel

that she's pleased, though she's not smiling or anything.

I shift from one foot to the other, then blurt, "You had a porcupine mouth." I giggle a nervous giggle.

"Yeah, I guess holding the pins in my mouth is not a good idea."

I sit cross-legged in front of her. Then she does a new thing — touches the top of my head. I smile at her.

She has a mole on her ankle. Seeing it, I touch it and remember a game we played when I was about two years old. "Mamma," I say, "Remember when I was little, I touched the mole on your ankle? And you pretended it hurt and said 'ouch.' Then I laughed. We did that over and over."

"I remember," she says. "Funny what amuses a small child."

"Mamma, do you remember anything from when you were small?" She leans back in her chair. Her eyes look backward into the past.

"I went to church every Sunday with my mamma and papa, just as you do. Back then, the men and boys sat on one side of the church, and the women and girls on the other. One Sunday — I think I was about three years old — I was sitting with my mamma …"

She pauses. Sits up straight and stiff.

"… well, Papa came over from his side and took my hand and we went outside. I smiled a big smile. I was so pleased to go out with Papa …"

Again Mamma stops. She looks so-o-o sad. Then mad, her mouth becoming a straight line. Smad.

"Well," she says, "when I came back into the church, I sure wasn't smiling anymore. My papa had spanked me and I didn't even know why. Maybe I was wiggling too much, or maybe I was making noise."

"Oh, Mamma. How awful!" I feel stunned. "Mamma, I'm sorry …"

"Well, that was a long time ago." She quickly turns back to her sewing. "I have to finish this dress." *RRRRR!*

***

I want to do something for Mamma. I decide to surprise her by making lunch. Hot dogs. Mamma buys hot dogs only for picnics — says they're not nutritious, but it's all I can think of right now. I close the kitchen door and move really quietly. I boil the hot dogs, cut up carrots, make a lettuce salad, find the hot dog buns, and set the table. Everything is ready, just as Mamma walks in holding up my finished, ugly, purple paisley dress.

Again her eyes open wide. "My, aren't you full of surprises today!" She stands looking at me as if deciding what to do. She walks towards me, then stops. I almost think she's going to hug me. I have a big wishing-wanting in my chest. I even take a step towards her. But she touches the top of my head instead. Hugging takes working up to.

Mamma doesn't complain about having hot dogs, though it's not a picnic. And I don't complain about the ugly, purple paisley dress.

I'll ask about jeans after lunch. For sure!

In the afternoon I help Mamma with the laundry. Papa's shirt waves from the line as I hang out clothes, and Mamma's bloomers — that's what she calls her underwear — blooms in the wind, puffing out like a big, pink flower. I giggle. I like the way the wind plays with the clothing, flapping and whipping it about. And I love the fresh smell. I put Mamma's damp apron against my face before pegging it to the line. The apron strap hangs close to the ground. Uh-oh! Here comes Stinker. She bats at the flapping apron strap. I move it to a higher line.

"I'm gonna ask Mamma for jeans," I tell Stinker who rubs around my legs, her rumbly motor purring. "But I gotta do it at the right time."

Just as I finish hanging the laundry, Mamma comes out of the house. "Rose, I need your help digging up the potatoes."

Mamma digs up clumps of potatoes with her spade. I take the potatoes from the holes, shake off the dirt, and put them into a bushel basket. I like how the dirt feels, damp and crumbly in my hands.

*Maybe now's the right time.* I take a deep breath. "Mamma …"

But along comes Daniel. "I wanna hewp." He pulls out some potatoes. Mostly he gets in the way.

"Mamma ..." I begin again.

But along comes Stinker. She peers into the potato hole. A tiny clump of dirt falls inside the hole. Seeing something move, Stinker pokes her paw into the hole, her ears forward.

"Stinker wants to hewp," says Daniel.

"Skedaddle!" Mamma waves Stinker away.

"Skedaddo ... skedaddo ... skedaddo," says Daniel.

"You too, you little *Schnickelfritz*," says Mamma. It's what she calls Daniel when he's being pesky, but she loves him anyway.

"*I'm* not a litto Schnicko-fritz." But he does skedaddle after Stinker.

I try again. "Ma — "

"*Ye-o-o-o-w!*" A horrible howl!

I look towards the clothesline where Papa's shirt is still waving, and Mamma's bloomers are still blooming. Uh-oh! Stinker's claws are caught on the strap of Mamma's apron. I didn't put it high enough.

"Shoo!" screeches Mamma running towards Stinker, the spade still in her hand. Stinker is tangled up in the apron, which rips off the line. Yowling and howling, she and the flapping apron stumble-tumble towards the barn, like a Halloween ghost. Oh my! I don't know whether to laugh or cry. It does look funny, but poor Stinker!

I go to the barn. Stinker is crouched in the corner, wild-eyed.

"It's okay, Stinker," I say in a soft voice. I go to her slowly. Gently, I unhook the terrible apron-monster from her claws.

\*\*\*

That's how the day goes. No time is the right time to ask Mamma about jeans.

*Finally*, after supper, Mamma sits and knits, her needles flying. It's almost bedtime, so it's now or never. I move close to her and sit cross-legged on the floor. She looks up, surprised, I think, that I've come so close.

"Mamma ... um ..." Tired of trying to figure out the right words, I just blurt it out. "Mamma, I need jeans because ..."

"You know how I feel about girls wearing boys' clothing."

"But Mamma, when I play at school, sometimes my dress flies up and that isn't at all *ladylike*."

"You go to school to learn, not to play."

"*Mamma!* What am I supposed to do at *recess?*" I don't want to tell her about falling in school, but I'm *desperate*. "Mamma, the other day we were playing ball and I fell and my *stupid* dress flew way up, probably way over my underpants, and ..." my voice gets higher "... *how ladylike is that?*" Oh no, I'm almost crying. In fact, a tiny sob strangles in my throat. Mamma looks startled. I can see she doesn't know what to do about my almost-crying. I have this crazy notion that she might get up and make some chicken soup or something. Sometimes she cooks me stuff when I'm upset. But today she sits quietly while I try to hold back hiccuppy sobs. If she were Aunt Bette, she'd hug me. But Mamma is Mamma. She gets up, and like the other day at the sewing machine, she touches the top of my head. And that's something.

That night when I'm in bed, Mamma passes my bedroom door. "I'll think about the jeans," she says.

# 9

## A Squirrel is a Squirrel

Soon it will be too cold to come to Grandmother
Oak. This might be the last time before spring.
Grandmother's leaves float down lazily — gold
against a blue autumn sky. With fewer leaves, it's
easier to see around me — dried corn stalks in the
neighbour's field. Bright splashes of colour —
orange pumpkins in our garden, trees of red,
yellow and orange. Drooping late sunflowers
dropping their seeds to grow again next year.

"Mamma said I can have jeans," I say to a chit-
ter-chatter squirrel in a branch above me.
"Whoop-de-do and hallelujah!" His chitter-chat-
ter gets louder. Guess he doesn't approve either.
Sure wish *someone* was on my side, besides Aunt

Bette. I lie back into the whisper-rippling leaves. A tiny spider drops and tickles its way across my hand onto a leaf. Why am I a girl, and why is the spider a spider? The world seems so strange sometimes and … and wonderful — if it weren't for Snooty Judy. Whoever thought up a spider? A squirrel? A person? The squirrel still scolds and stares. It seems somehow … not real, almost, that I'm sitting in this tree, at this moment, staring at a squirrel. Am I real? Is the squirrel real? The tree? Maybe it's a dream.

And then I hear a small voice, "I see you, Rose." Daniel is peering up into the tree. Well, real or not, I climb down to Daniel. I love him. That feels real.

"I got wots and wots of acorns!" He's gathered a whole pile.

"Uh-huh, lots and lots." I pick one up and rub it — so smooth. "See the little cap it wears?" Daniel giggles. "Wait here, Daniel," I say, and run into the house to get a pencil. Back outside, I draw a happy face on the acorn. I hold the acorn face in front of me and ask, "How do you know to grow into an oak tree instead of an elm or a maple?" I throw the acorn head to Daniel. "Catch!" He reaches awkwardly and misses. Reminds me of how I used to try catching a softball. I'm a bit better now. I've been practising. Daniel looks at the acorn face and laughs. "I wanna make one."

I give him the pencil. He squishes up his face and chews on his bottom lip as he tries to draw a face. "I *can't*" he wails, making a pouty face. "You do it."

"When you're as big as I am, you'll be able to do it just fine." I make him a sad-faced acorn.

"Why is she sad?"

"Because someone is mean to her."

"Oh!" He frowns. "Why is the other one happy?"

"Because she has a spunky little brother named Daniel."

Giggling, Daniel throws himself onto a whole pile of crackle-crunch leaves and wiggles about. He knows how to be happy with his whole body.

I make him lots of acorn faces — scared ones and mad ones, surprised ones and smad ones.

Daniel puts his acorn people in a row. "I'm gonna teach you a song," he says. *"You put your right foot in. You take your right foot out."*

Another camp song I taught him. After a minute, Daniel stops and looks at the little line of faces.

"But the acorn peep-o got no feet. How can they do the hokey-pokey?"

"You gotta pretend."

"Okay. *You do the hokey-pokey and you turn yourself around.*"

Daniel and the acorn people are getting along just fine, so I go back to my own thoughts.

"Hey!" Suddenly a yelp from Daniel. "That squirr-o took my acorn." A squirrel dashes away with one of Daniel's acorn people. Daniel's face is red and his lips poke out.

"Maybe he'll help an oak tree grow."

"He's *not* hewping … he took …"

"Look Daniel." I point to the squirrel who is burying the acorn. Daniel's pout slowly turns into a smile. "An acorn is a seed for an oak tree."

"Reewy?"

"Uh-huh. Really. Squirrels bury acorns for food. But lots of times they forget about their buried acorns. Then a baby tree might grow. I learned that in a tree book at school."

"If the squirr-o forgets, wiw a the tree grow?"

"Maybe."

Daniel hunches over and walks very slowly towards the squirrel. He gets quite close, then squats watching, a beaming smile on his face.

I hope the squirrel forgets. I imagine the baby tree growing and dropping acorns for other trees to grow — Grandmother Oak's grandchildren. Oak tree grandchildren, not human like me. I smile to myself. And those oak grandchildren will have grandchildren, and on and on. But all those grandchildren will take about a *gazillion* years, because the tree book says that oak trees don't grow acorns until they're about 20 years old or more. And oak trees live to be two hundred years old or even more.

As I think about the foreverness of acorns and oak trees, Daniel comes to me, his acorn people forgotten.

"Wook, Rose." On his arm is a butterfly, orange and black, one of his favourite critters. Its wings slowly open and close. We watch it for I don't know how long. Then, all at once, it flits away and is gone.

"Aw," says Daniel. "I wish we could have keeped it."

"Butterflies are not for keeping," I say.

"Why?"

I don't know how to answer him. Finally I say, "They have to fly to their own places."

We think our own thoughts for a while. Then I say, "Daniel, do you ever wonder why you were born a boy and not a butterfly or a squirrel or something else?"

"I'm not a butterfwy. I'm not a squirr-o. I'm a boy and a squirr-o is a squirr-o," he says firmly.

Well, it seems Daniel isn't in a mood for thinking about the why of things, so I join his thoughts instead.

"A girl is a girl," I say, "and a squirrel is a squirrel."

"A gir-o is a gir-o, and a squirr-o is a squirr-o."

Then he adds, "A worm is a … *worm!*" He says worm the second time in a high, squeaky voice.

"A worm is a *worm!*" I copy Daniel's *Dummheit* and say worm the second time in a squeaky voice.

Again, Daniel rolls giggling in the rustling, golden leaves.

The nice thing about having a little brother is that sometimes it lets me be four-year-old silly. Maybe I have a way with little kids. Maybe I'll be a kindergarten teacher. Or an eccentric aunt. Or something completely different. A truck driver.

With Daniel dancing behind me, I skip about, chanting,

"A squirrel is a *squirrel.*

A tree is a *tree.*

And I, by golly, am *me.*"

Then I stop. "Don't tell Mamma I said golly," I say. I'm not sure whether it is an almost-curse.

Daniel puts his face nose-to-nose with mine. "Are we in cahoots?" he whispers.

"Yeah," I say, "with a hint of mirth."

# 10

## Yet Another Doll

I want a softball glove for Christmas. But I always get a doll. Every single year. I'm too old for a doll. But I'll get one anyway. I've already seen my doll. Mamma always buys the next year's doll during the after-Christmas sales. And she always hides it in the same place — on the top closet shelf in the upstairs spare bedroom. It didn't take long to figure that out — just a little poking around. Shortly after last Christmas, I did my first doll viewing. Viewing. That's what they called it when my Great Aunt Olga died, and people went to see her lying in the coffin. Come to think of it, the long, narrow doll box looks sort of like a coffin.

I decide to have another look now, mostly because I'm bored. In the upstairs spare bedroom closet, I pull up a chair and open the box. The doll has a ruffly, yellow dress and a matching bonnet. I hate ruffles. She does look a bit like my great aunt in her coffin — fancy clothes and the same stiff smile. I giggle. I lift her out of the box.

"Waaah!" she wails when I tilt her backwards.

"Shhh," I whisper. "Do you want to get me in trouble?" I close the closet door. I tilt her up and lay her back a few times. Each time, one long, thin wail, sort of like a cat's meow.

"What do you think of being shut up in this box when there's a whole, big world out there?" I ask.

"Waaah!"

"I feel that way too sometimes. What do you think about me getting a doll every single year when I really want a softball glove?"

"Waaah!"

"I agree, but it has nothing to do with you personally."

Putting the dolly aside, I imagine a softball

glove on my right hand. I punch my fist into the glove. *Thwack!* I smell the leathery smell. I am the shortstop at a spring ball game. *Crack!* The batter hits the ball which zooms towards me. *Smack!* Right into my glove. I whiz the ball to first base where the runner, *oh I do believe it's Snooty Judy*, is out! Wild cheers from my teammates.

"Come set the table for supper." Mamma's voice jerks me out of my dream.

I sigh. "I'm afraid there'll be no softball glove for Christmas," I say to the doll as I lay her back into her coffin-box.

"Waaah!"

As I come into the kitchen, I pretend I don't know about the doll. "Know what I want for Christmas?" I say.

Papa is sitting in the corner, reading *The Farm Journal*. Maybe he'll take pity. What if I get a doll *and* a softball glove? Doesn't hurt to try.

"I'm afraid it's too late for Christmas requests," says Mamma.

I ignore this and say, "I *really, really, really* need a softball glove." I glance at Papa.

"A softball glove? *Dummheit!*" says Mamma. "You've already spent far too much time throwing that ball around. First you want jeans so you can prance around shamelessly in boys' clothing. And now you want a softball glove. Where will it end?"

"But Mamma, I need to learn to play ball as well as the other kids. They laugh at kids who don't know how to play. Besides, Aunt Bette said I have a natural ability."

"Let them laugh. You need to learn the important things, like cooking, cleaning, and making good grades. As for natural ability, Aunt Bette has a natural ability for putting notions into your head."

"What's natur-o abiwity?" asks Daniel.

Papa, laying *The Farm Journal* aside, stands up and comes towards us. "Natural ability. Being good at a specific thing. Rose has a natural ability for softball." He winks at me. "And you, Daniel, have a natural ability with critters — animals, insects, and such." Daniel beams. "And Mamma here … she is a master chef … and I think she is

73

hiding other talents too numerous to mention."
Mamma stares at him, mouth hanging open.
Then a hint of a smile. I wonder about Mamma's
abilities, too numerous to mention.

# 11

## Jeans Shopping

Mamma and I walk into JC Penney's department store.

"Can I help you?" asks the saleslady in a clippity voice. She is all cityfied, with bright red lipstick, dangle-jangle earrings, clickety-clack heels, and a tight-in-the-behind, blue dress.

"We came to shop for jeans for Rose," says Mamma.

The saleslady raises one eyebrow. She looks me over, top to bottom. I feel myself blush.

"This way." She clickity-clacks ahead of us. The seams on her nylon stockings are perfectly straight. Her tight, blue behind wiggles.

There are racks of jeans, and racks of other

girls' pants — blue, green, and, *oh no*, pink. Mamma goes to the rack of coloured pants.

"Mamma, *jeans!* I need *jeans!*"

"But these are much more ladylike. The jeans are so boyish."

The saleslady has a smirky little smile. I wish she'd stop hovering. Mamma takes the pink pants off the rack. Holds them out, her head to one side.

I have to think of something quick. "Mamma, the jeans are much more *sensible* and *durable*. They'll last forever."

"Well, jeans may be more durable, but you'll grow out of them in no time anyway. Just try these on." She holds the awful pink pants towards me.

"Mamma, *please*. Don't make me try the pink ones. I'll try the blue ones." I'm brave enough to add, "… but I'm going to try the durable jeans, too."

She agrees, with a sigh.

*Finally*, the saleslady leaves, as I take the blue pants and several sizes of jeans into the dressing room. First I try the blue pants, to keep Mamma happy. Maybe they won't fit. I hope! I hope! I hope!

They fit.

"Perfect," says Mamma.

"Oh Mamma, *please!* See how thin the material is. If I fall down just once, they'll tear. Jeans would be much better." I see myself sliding into home base and these silly pants ripping wide open. Of course, I don't say anything to Mamma about sliding into home base. She'd forbid me from softball forever.

"Well," says Mamma, "try on the jeans if you must."

I try on the ones I like best. I come out of the dressing room to look in the mirror. I turn this way and that. I love the way they kind of hug my legs and hips.

"They're perfect, Mamma."

"Oh no! They're *much* too tight."

The saleslady clickity-clacks towards us again, that I'm-better-than-you smile still on her face. I think she is enjoying this whole thing. I imagine her going home and telling her whole family about this quaint Mennonite mother and daughter who came in to buy jeans. I feel like smacking

her smirking face — a very un-Mennonite thing
to do. But I feel so embarrassed as Mamma goes
on and on about the tight jeans.

"No daughter of mine will wear *those!*"

I try on a bigger size.

"Much better," says Mamma

"Too big," I say. But I agree to get these. If I
don't, Mamma might change her mind about
jeans altogether. She'd buy those blue pants — or
worse, the pink ones.

# 12

## A Whole New Person

Even though I've wanted jeans forever, I'm scared to wear them to school. What will the kids think about me all at once showing up in jeans? They think my dresses are goofy, but they're used to it. Maybe now they'll laugh at my jeans. But my new clothes are part of being a new person. I think of that sermon where Jesus talked to Nicodemus about being a whole new person ... though Jesus didn't mean Nicodemus should wear jeans. I laugh at the funny picture in my head of Nicodemus in jeans. Anyway, it's time to go to school, and I can't decide whether to wear my jeans. Maybe I'll be a whole new person tomorrow. But I look at my camp photo beside my bed. "Okay," I say to that girl. "I'll do it."

Sure enough, when I get to school, Judy points and hoots, "Hey everybody, look at Rose. Guess she thinks she's really something with her *jeans*! Well it takes more than jeans. You're still a Lone Tree loser. Besides your jeans are way too baggy. Baggy butt! Baggy butt!"

Though my jeans are a bit too big, they're not *that* baggy.

I hurt inside, but I look her right in the eye.

"Baggy butt," she says again, but her voice isn't as loud this time. "What're you staring at?"

I still don't look away — even take a step towards her. And wonder of wonders, she turns away.

"I'm getting outa here," she says. "You're not worth it." Finding someone else to torment, she goes to Sandra. Gives her a little push, and then storms away.

No one else says anything bad about my jeans. One kid, Cindy, even says she likes them.

After recess Mr. Ford says, "I have something important to tell you." Kids rustle their books and shuffle their feet. I wonder if it's really important or just a dumb old math test or something.

"Prairie View School is going to put on a play — *Anne of Green Gables*."

Everyone is suddenly quiet. A whisper of excitement stirs the air. There is a big *whoosh* in my belly, then things go kind of quiet inside me. A voice in my head whispers *I'm going to try out for Anne*.

But that's crazy! I'm way too shy, and kids might laugh. Oh! I almost forgot. A whole new person doesn't think that way. I straighten up, and again hear that voice in my head: *I'm going to try out for Anne*.

I'm *not* going to try out for Diana, who doesn't have much imagination. I'm *not* going to try out for nosey Mrs. Lynde. I am *not* going to try out for stern-faced Marilla, who thinks fun stuff is *Dummheit*.

I'm going to try out for the spunkiest part of all — Anne. Never mind what the other kids think.

"We will have tryouts next week," says Mr. Ford. "Sign up for the part you want. If you have a second choice, put that down, too. We will give you a piece from your chosen characters to practise, but at the tryouts we may also ask you to read other parts from your characters. You have till the day after tomorrow to sign up for the parts of your choice. Of course, we'll also need people to help with the props."

I'm not going to give a second choice. I only want to be Anne.

Walking home with Sandra, I ask, "Are you going to try out for the play?"

"No!" she says firmly. Then a second later, she smiles. "Maybe I'll help out with the props. Are you going to try out, Rose?"

"Yeah," I say, using a new, sure voice, "I want to play Anne."

She stops walking. Stares at me. "Do you think you'd be good at *that?*"

Her words grind in my belly. "Yes!" I shout. "Why does everyone think I'm stupid? Even you. And why do you keep bringing those stupid, stinky sandwiches to school?" *Why am I, all at once, yelling about sandwiches?* But I can't stop.

"You're just asking for it from Judy. And those sandwiches *are* stinky, stinky, stinky!"

Sandra surprises me "I *like* those sandwiches." She lifts her head. "I *won't* stop bringing them."

It's the first time I've seen her sort of … spunky. I'm not so mad anymore, but I'm not quite ready to forgive her. We walk quietly.

Finally, hearing Aunt Bette's words coming from my mouth, I say, "Good for you. I mean about not letting Judy stop you from bringing your sandwiches."

Sandra smiles, gives her head a firm little nod. "Yeah! I have a half sandwich left. You want a taste?" She bends down and takes the sandwich from her lunchbox. Hands it to me.

I sniff, wrinkle my nose. "Phew!"

I take a tiny bite. Not bad, actually.

Another bite. The strong, sharp cheese, together with her mamma's homemade rye bread is really pretty good. I close my eyes and chew. "Mmm. Stink-alicious!" We both laugh. "Next time Snooty Judy bugs you about your sandwich, wave it under her nose."

She giggles. "Yeah! Um … Rose?"

"Yeah?"

"You'd probably do really good with the Anne part."

I smile. "Sorry I yelled at you, Sandra."

# 13

## Practice in the Hayloft

I'm practising my *Anne of Green Gables* script in
the hayloft of our barn. The hayloft is my winter
thinking place — when it's too cold for
Grandmother Oak,

"I hate you! I hate you! I hate you!" I yell to
the imagined Mrs. Lynde. It's the part where Mrs.
Lynde visits and says Anne is skinny and homely
and has hair as red as carrots. Stinker, sleeping on
a pile of hay, wakes up and looks at me with big,
scared eyes. "Not you, Stinker. I don't hate you. I
hate Mrs. Lynde ... and Snooty Judy," I mumble.
"Sorry, God. I know I'm suppose to love everyone, but it sure is hard. Couldn't You maybe make
certain people nicer?" I look back at my script.

Scrunching up my forehead, I make my eyes blaze, like it says in the script. "How *dare* you call me skinny and homely?" I shout.

Stinker zooms to a hiding place behind a bale of hay.

I sigh. "Stinker, how can I practise when you take everything personally. I'm not mad at *you!* Well, I'm sorry, but I have to learn my lines." I clench my fist and stamp my foot. "How would you like having horrible things said about you, Mrs. Lynde?"

Stinker zips right out the door.

"And same to you, Snooty Judy. Who do you think you are? You are *rude*! And probably don't have a spark of imagination. I don't care if I hurt your feelings. I hope I hurt them. You have hurt mine *excruciatingly*! I feel *smurt, smurt, smurt!*"

Okay, so I didn't exactly stick to the script. But that yelling kinda feels good in the guts.

I know I'm supposed to be a good Christian and a good Mennonite and forgive Judy, but those nasty thoughts keep popping into my head. Actually though, things are a bit better between

Judy and me since I stared her down, that day I came to school in jeans. She hasn't been quite as nasty.

Stinker peeks in the door, her eyes still wide. "It's safe to come in now," I say in a soft voice. She comes slowly forward, her eyes never leaving my face. She stops just before she gets to me.

"It's okay," I murmur. "I'm finished shouting at Mrs. Lynde." She jumps onto my lap. She has forgiven me. She's a better Mennonite than I am. I settle down to practise my script — quietly, inside my head, this time.

# 14

## Quiet Doesn't Mean Stupid

Play tryouts today, right after opening exercises. I don't feel like a whole new person. I just feel scared.

We stand for the Lord's Prayer.

*Our Father, who art in heaven … Thy will be done …"*

Is getting into the play Thy will, or only mine? Maybe You don't care one way or another. My Sunday school teacher talked about doing God's will, and not our own.

*… Give us this day our daily bread …*

You don't even have to worry about the daily bread. Just please, please, please help me through the tryouts.

*… Lead us not into temptation …*

I'm tempted to not even try out after all. I could just say I changed my mind.

*… For ever and ever amen.*

Mrs. Gibbons marches into the room when the amen is barely finished. "Time to get started. I'll call you in one at a time. We'll start with the Anne part." *Oh Help!* There's three of us trying out — Cindy, Karen, and me. "Cindy, you first."

I'm so glad I'm not first, but disappointed at the same time. Sure would like to get this over with. My heart hammers, and I don't even realize my hands are tapping my desk until Mr. Ford gently puts his hand over mine and smiles at me. Other kids look scared, too — eyes open wide, pale faces, swinging legs.

"This is not a death sentence," says Mr. Ford. "Only tryouts. Have fun with it."

Easy for him to say.

"Stand up everyone," he says. "Let's sing *The Grand Old Duke of York.*"

*The grand old duke of York,*
*He had ten thousand men.*

*He marched them up to the top of the hill*
*And he marched them down again.*

*And when they were up, they were up;*
*And when they were down, they were down.*
*And when they were only halfway up,*
*They were neither up nor down!*

We do all the sitting down and standing up motions, though we have to sit sideways in our desks to do it. I know Mr. Ford is trying to calm our jittery-twitters. I imagine those ten thousand men having play tryouts and the duke of York tries to calm them by marching them up and down the hill. What if I said this out loud? Often I think of jokes in my head, but never *ever* say them out loud. A whole new person probably would. Yeah, a little joke to go with my jeans. Thinking about saying it out loud starts my heart boom-booming again. I can't do it. I have enough heart hammerings just thinking about tryouts. But then the strangest thing happens, as if God or a guardian angel was giving me another chance.

Tom pipes up, "How come they marched up the hill, then marched back down for no reason? Sounds pretty stupid to me."

Not letting my thumpity-bump heart stop me, I blurt, "They probably had tryouts for some huge play, and the grand old duke of York was trying to help them feel calm."

A big, booming laugh bursts out of Mr. Ford. "Yes, Rose has it figured out."

Some kids laugh, but Snooty Judy glares at me. I stare back. I think Judy wants me to be quiet and stupid forever. *But I did a joke!* And some kids laughed.

"Rose, you're next." I hadn't even seen Mrs. Gibbons come in.

I follow Mrs. Gibbons into the staff room, the only empty room for tryouts. Two other teachers are there too. I wish one of them was Mr. Ford. My head is still busy with what just happened. I don't feel as nervous as I did, but it's hard to concentrate with ten thousand men marching in my head. Go away, I say to them. I imagine Mrs. Lynde in front of me instead.

"I hate you! I hate you! I hate you!" I yell. I go through all the parts. I glare and stamp, and shout. "How would *you* like to have horrible things said about you?" I'm hardly nervous at all anymore. It's soon over and I sigh a big, whooshing sigh. Well, maybe I was a *bit* nervous. The three teachers laugh. I blush. Hardly seems fair. Three of them and one of me.

"That was very good," says Mrs. Gibbons, "though these decisions are often very difficult. The results will be on the bulletin board tomorrow."

*Very good* she said. I wonder if she says that to everyone. Well, I think I did well.

Oooh! I really, really, really want this! Tomorrow, please hurry along.

***

The time has come. I stand in a crowd of pushing, shoving kids in front of the bulletin board, which has the list of who is in the play. My heart is hammering. I can't believe I want this *s-o-o-o* badly.

The crowd pushes me closer. Almost there. I strain my neck — can't see yet. But then I spot Snooty Judy's name … well it doesn't say "snooty" on the list. She whoops. I squint and strain my eyes. I see other names — Tom, Norman. Finally, I'm there. I look down the list. I don't see my name. I look more carefully.

My name isn't there! Cindy's is. She got the part of Anne.

Snooty Judy sticks her pointy nose in the air and hisses, "Get out of the way, loser. *You're* not on the list." She is back to being just as nasty as ever. I am not a whole new person anymore. I can't face Judy today.

I shuffle away. I bite my bottom lip. I will *not* cry. From the corner of my eye, I see Mr. Ford looking at me — something on his face — pity? Oh no! *He feels sorry for me.* I turn away quickly and hurry to class. I don't pay any attention all through stupid math. Other kids' hands fly up when Mr. Ford asks questions, even if they don't know the answer. I don't raise my hand even when I do know the answer. Maybe even the teachers think I'm stupid, because I don't raise my hand often, or because I'm quiet. I'll bet that's why I didn't get into the play. They think I'm not good at *anything!*

Finally, school is over. I try to slip out without talking to anyone. No such luck.

Mr. Ford says, "Rose, may I see you for a minute?" I go up to his desk, not looking at his face. I know he is still feeling sorry for me.

"Would you like to help with props for the play?" Mr. Ford's voice is soft. "Mrs. Gibson tells me that Sandra is painting a backdrop. Maybe she could use some help."

I want to yell, *No I don't want to help with stupid props! I want to be in the play. Can't you see that I could have done a great job even if I'm quiet? Quiet doesn't mean stupid!*

But all I say is "no" and I shuffle out.

# 15

## Heinrich and Harry

When I get home, I sneak to the hayloft before chores. I fling myself into a haypile. Smad! Not chosen again. Smurt! Those stupid teachers won't *let* me be a whole new person. They won't *let* me be Anne. Thinking these angry thoughts again. "But I'm doing the best I can!" I yell this to God, and he doesn't strike me dead.

Aunt Bette is coming over for supper and I'm not even glad. Tonight of all nights! Usually, I love seeing her, but today I don't want to talk to anyone.

At supper I barely eat, even though we are having what I usually like best — Mamma's crunchy-scrumptious fried chicken, mashed potatoes, gravy, and green beans. I think Daniel knows I'm in the dumps, 'cause he keeps watching me, his eyes big. "Rose, don't you want some smashed potatoes?" His way of saying mashed potatoes. Maybe he wants to fix things with food, like Mamma does sometimes.

"No smashed potatoes today, Daniel."

Mamma squints at me. "Isn't today the day you found out about the play?"

"Yeah, I didn't get in." I say it as though I don't care. I even shrug.

"Oh."

I poke at my green beans with my fork, moving them around on my plate.

"Well maybe now you'll finally buckle down to school work."

My belly grinds. How dare she say such a thing? I stab a green bean.

"All this *Dumm* ..."

I've heard this all before, but today I can't listen. I push my chair back so hard it falls over. Pretending I don't care is definitely not working. I bite my bottom lip to keep the crying in, and dash to the hayloft.

"Rose?" Mamma's voice sounds surprised. "Come back."

"Let her go," says Papa.

In the hayloft I shout at Mamma, though she isn't there. "How could you *say* that? Don't you know I wanted to be Anne more than *anything?* Don't you care how I *feel?* You don't want me to have any *fun!*"

I plunk in the hay, kind of half-sobbing. I wrap my arms around myself in a hug.

After a while I hear the barn door open. I peek. It's Aunt Bette. I hold my sobbing in and stare into my lap.

"I wanted to give you some time alone, but I wonder if it's okay if I join you now?"

I shrug. "I guess."

She sits beside me. "You wanna talk about it?"

"*No!*" Oops! That came out awfully mad. Well, I am mad! "Know what I think? A person can't be Mennonite and spunky at the same time." I peek up at Aunt Bette who tries to cover a smile.

"You sure look spunky now," she says.

"Mamma won't *let* me be spunky. She didn't

97

even want me to be in the play. She doesn't want me to play ball. She doesn't want me to have *any* fun — just study and behave and be quiet every single minute ... and be religious." Aunt Bette stays quiet, but I sure don't. "And those stupid teachers. I think I didn't get into the play because I'm quiet in class. Maybe even because ... because I'm Mennonite ... well maybe not, but still, maybe they think I'm just all-around strange and stupid *because* I'm Mennonite."

She just sits a while. Then says, "Wanna sit in my lap, darlin'?"

"Aunt *Bette!* I'm nine years *old!* "

"Never too old for a little cuddle. I sure need a hug from time to time."

She opens her arms and I climb in — my skinny legs sticking out. Her lap feels all soft and pillowey. Sinking in, my sobs burst out. She rocks me as if I was a little kid, and she makes hummy-murmury sounds. I don't even care that I'm nine years old. I leak tears and snot all over her blouse, for I don't know how long. Finally, I say in a chokey voice, "I wanted to be Anne of Green Gables."

"Mmm … I know darlin'." Again she is quiet for a while, then says, "I'd say it was awfully spunky to try out."

I think about this. "Yeah, I was really, really scared," I say in a wobbly voice, "but I did it anyway."

"You know, Rose, I never had it in me to try out for things — plays, choirs, and such."

*"Really?"* I am amazed. "I thought you weren't scared of anything."

"Well, I can ham it up with the best of them. But to get up on a stage, in front of folks I don't know? That's another matter. I don't mind leaving the spotlight to others. Now, your *Mamma* was very good at drama."

"No!" I simply can't believe it. Again I'm amazed. "I thought it would be the other way around — you good at drama and Mamma not wanting to try out. Oh, I remember Papa saying once that Mamma had abilities too numerous to mention."

"Well, that's one of them. Your Mamma did readings very well, but her papa, your grandpa was hard on her — didn't let her go to literary evenings or encourage her to develop her ability. And your Mamma had to work so hard — had to look after her little sister — me — and that couldn't have been easy."

I laugh. "Poor Mamma, chasing naughty little Bette."

"So, you wonder whether Mennonites can be spunky?"

"Yeah!"

"Don't you think your eccentric aunt is just a tiny bit spunky, even though she was afraid to try out for plays and such?"

"Yeah, but you aren't like a real Mennonite."

"Oh, I'm Mennonite alright. Not that I didn't think of looking elsewhere for my faith when I was younger. But I decided to bloom where I was planted."

"Why did you decide to … to bloom where you were planted?"

"You know darlin', I love these Menno-folks — got good hearts, most of them, and they're honest, fair. But Rose, you ask the right questions. Keeps me on my toes." She gets up and does a little tippy-toe dance, not at all like other folks around here. *"Wheee!"* She holds her long orange skirt above her knees. Her dangly earrings jangle. Hay dust flurries around her.

I laugh and join her. *"Dummheit! Dummheit! Dummheit!"*

"Isn't *Dummheit* fun?" she asks.

We plop back into our straw nest both giggling like little kids.

"Achoo!"

"Anyway," says Aunt Bette, "I decided to stay Mennonite because I greatly respect ..." her voice becomes serious and quiet, "well ... some Mennonite ideas, especially that war is not the way to solve differences. I believe very strongly that war just makes more wars. Just like in a schoolyard when Heinrich hits Harry, then Harry hits Heinrich back, then Heinrich hits Harry, and on and on. It never stops."

"Who are Heinrich and Harry?"

"I made them up, but I've seen the Heinrich-Harry story plenty of times."

"What are Heinrich and Harry supposed to *do* rather than hitting each other?"

"What do *you* think?"

"Maybe Harry could find a way of helping Heinrich feel better … or something… rather than hitting back?"

"Maybe."

"But *I* think if Harry didn't hit back, he'd just get beaten up," I say.

"Maybe he would. That's why being Mennonite takes spunk, and courage. But spunk never hangs its head. I was just reading today about a woman who set up an orphanage for Jewish children in France during the recent horrible war — World War II. Come to think of it, I can lend you the book, which tells about many brave Mennonites, some who were even killed because of their beliefs. And right now there are lots of Menno-folks working all over the world for the Mennonite Central Committee — working in schools, hospitals, farms, and such. But darlin' I've already done enough speechifying for today." She hugs me once more and looks at me the way I wish Mamma would, her eyes sort of soft, then leaves.

A couple of seconds later, she pokes her head back in. "Just one other thing I want to mention. I wonder if there is a way of finding out why you didn't get into the play."

I stay in the hayloft a bit longer after Aunt Bette leaves. Stinker comes in — settles into a furry-purry ball in my lap. I think about Heinrich and Harry, and Judy and me — Sandra, too. And about the play. Maybe not getting in doesn't mean I didn't do well. Maybe Cindy and I *both* did well. What would be a brave thing to do now? Maybe I could ask Mrs. Gibbons how I could have done better. Nah, I don't think I could do that. Or could I? Oooh my belly feels wibbly-wobbly thinking about talking to her. I have the rest of the weekend to think about it.

# 16

## Spunk Doesn't Hang Its Head

Monday morning. I've decided to talk to Mrs. Gibbons about the tryouts. And I gotta face Judy. Just when things were getting a bit better between us, she has this to bug me about. Well there's no help for it. I go to school.

Sure enough, she kinda edges up to me. "Too bad there isn't a donkey in the play. You could have tried out for that — maybe the back end of the donkey."

I feel too bad to stare her down like I did the other time — I know my lips would tremble or something. I turn away, but lift my head high and walk away as proudly as I can. *Spunk never hangs its head.*

On the way to class I see Mrs. Gibbons coming down the hallway. *Maybe talking to her is a dumb idea*, says a voice in my head. *It's what I decided to do*, says another voice. Oh dear, she's walking in a clippity, hurry-worry way. I don't think she even sees me. Though my belly does a flip-flop, I blurt out, "Um, Mrs. Gibbons?"

"Do you want something, Rose?" *Yeah, I sure do, but you wouldn't give it to me.* Out loud I say, "I was wondering whether, um … I could talk to you about something."

She glances at her watch. "Okay, Rose. I can take a few minutes. Actually, I want to talk to you, too. Let's go see whether that's okay with Mr. Ford." She comes with me to the classroom. "Can you spare Rose for a few minutes?" she asks.

"Guess we can manage for a few minutes, but our class can't do without her for long." He smiles at me. Mr. Ford is the *best* teacher. Mrs. Gibbons and I go to the staff room.

"What is it, Rose?"

My throat feels dry. What if this is a stupid

thing to do? What if she thinks I'm whining? But I take a deep breath and say. "I was wondering if you could tell me … maybe … what I could have done better … at the tryouts, I mean … and why I didn't get the part."

"Oh Rose, I'm glad you asked."

I feel a lot better already. Asking isn't stupid.

"Actually that's exactly what I wanted to talk to you about. You did *very* well, Rose. I didn't know you had such a *big* voice. I wish you'd use it more."

*Oh! Oh! Oh! I did good!*

"It was a hard decision. We really did consider you. I have no doubt you could have done a good job. In the end, though, we chose Cindy. One suggestion, Rose. At a few places your voice was a bit high pitched. Keep your voice big — strong, as you did for the most part, but remember that a lower voice is stronger than a high-pitched voice."

*Sure wish someone had told me that before tryouts.* Still, I feel a tiny glow in my belly. Though I can't be in the play, *I did good!* Maybe it's even another natural ability.

"I wish you'd have given a second choice," says Mrs. Gibbons. "Maybe we could have used you for another part. I'm sure we'll do another play next year. Be sure to try again."

"Thanks, Mrs. Gibbons." I feel so glowy inside that something else pops out of my mouth before I hardly think about it. "I can help with props."

"Why, Rose, that's wonderful! You can help Sandra with the backdrop."

As I go into the classroom, I'm actually smiling. Judy looks at me, but my smile doesn't stop.

# 17

## Not the King of the World

"I think that looks real good," I say to Sandra. I never knew she was so good at drawing stuff. She and I are working on the backdrop after school. Trees and a house with green gables. Sandra does all the sketching and I help paint.

Judy comes by. "What's *that?*" she asks, pointing to a tree that Sandra has just painted. "It looks like the hind end of a horse."

Sandra doesn't say anything. I stand up, look Judy right in the eye and say, "I think it looks *exactly* like a tree — a very good tree."

"It looks like a horse's butt," Judy says, and marches away.

Though I have thumpety-bumping heart

because I'm new at standing up to folks, I feel good 'cause I *did* it.

"Who ever heard of a *green* horse's butt?" mumbles Sandra, looking at her tree.

"Maybe you could make an orange horse's butt for autumn," I say. Sandra giggles.

"Judy thinks she's the king of the world." Sandra grumbles more than she used to. "I don't feel like working anymore," she says. "Let's go home."

"I'll bet Judy's just jealous that she can't draw like you."

Sandra is already putting stuff away. And I have to get home to chores — promised Mamma I'd stay only a half hour after school.

As we walk home, Sandra's bottom lip pokes out, like Daniel's when he's mad.

"Judy can't even tell the difference between a tree and a horse's butt," I say. Sandra's pouty face turns into a smile. Thinking about Heinrich and Harry, I wonder about making fun of Judy, but I'm helping Sandra feel better.

"She's *not* the king of the world," I say.

Sandra joins me.

"She's *not* the king of the world." We chant together, laughing.

I use my bag of books as a sort of drum, and add to the rhythm.

"She's *not* the king of the world." PUM-PUM! Sandra copies the rhythm.

When I beat the rhythm on my books, I notice that my book bag doesn't seem heavy enough for my math and spelling books. I look in. My spelling book isn't there! I groan. "Sandra, my spelling book isn't in my bag. Where did I …? Oh! I think I left it on the side steps of the school. I set it down to tie my shoe."

"We have a test tomorrow," she says.

"I *know*. You go on home. I have to go back. I might be in trouble for getting home late, but I'll be in bigger trouble if I lose my spelling book."

Back at the school, sure enough, there is my spelling book on the side-door steps. What a relief! Slipping it into my bag, I hear a strange sound. Snuffling! Someone is crying. Sounds like it's coming from behind the school. Who is it? I better go see what's the matter, though my pitter-patter heart doesn't want to. I peek around the corner, then jerk my head back so quickly, I scrape my cheek on the corner of the school-house. *Ouch.*

*It's Judy!*

I can't make my brain believe it. Tough Judy, hunched and sobbing. It doesn't make sense. Carefully, I peek again. It's her alright. She looks so small and sad. Well, I'm *not* going to her! I'm having a hard enough time trying to make things better between us. If I go to her now, she'll just hate me more than ever, 'cause I guess she doesn't want anyone to see her crying. I turn to go home. But I don't walk away. My mind is a muddled tangle. Heinrich and Harry are tumbling about in my brain. *Maybe Harry could help Heinrich feel better.* Do I really believe that? But my crazy feet take me slowly around the corner of the building, though my heart is putt-putting louder than our tractor. There she sits, sniffling. She doesn't see me at first. She sure doesn't look like the king of the world. All at once, I'm not afraid. But I don't know what to do or say, so I just stand there. Finally she sees me and yells, "What are *you* doing here?"

Ignoring her question, I ask, "What's the matter Judy?"

"None of your business!" she yells. "Stop staring! And if you tell *anyone*, you're dead!" She gets up. Comes towards me. Pushes me against the wall. Hard.

That does it. A fire in my belly explodes and I push her right back. *"You're not the king of the world,"* I roar. Judy sprawls to the ground. My legs are trembling. I'm shaking all over. Judy gets up and runs past me towards home.

Stunned, I go too. I just failed the Heinrich-and-Harry test — in a big way. I feel shivery all the way home, though it's not even very cold.

# 18

## Out of the Shadows

"Practice in just five minutes," says Mr. Ford, "for those of you in the play." A little jealous grind twists in my belly. But just a couple of days ago it was a *huge* grind. "Sandra, you and Rose can work on the backdrop during practice. It's coming along really well. You have a real talent." He smiles a big smile at Sandra.

Judy comes past as we work. "You have a real talent," she says in a nasty, high voice. "Well, that tree still looks like a horse's behind to me."

Sandra doesn't answer — just keeps working. Judy just stares at the backdrop. I think even she can see that Sandra is a great drawer. But she finds another way to be nasty. "Did you bring your stinky sandwiches?"

"Yeah, you want some?" I can't believe it — Sandra speaking up to Judy.

"Are you kidding?" Judy stomps away.

I grin at Sandra. She has a tiny smile.

"She isn't mean to you anymore," says Sandra. It's true. She hasn't been nasty to me since I saw her crying — just ignores me. I wonder why she was crying. Maybe things are bad at her house. I saw her papa once when he picked her up from school. He had a big, mean-looking scowl, sort of the same as Judy's.

"What do you think I should do about Snooty Judy?" Sandra asks. Now Sandra is calling her Snooty Judy! Somehow, I don't feel like calling her that anymore — not since the crying. And it feels funny that Sandra is asking me what to do. I'm trying to figure it out myself, for goodness sakes. I keep seeing the picture in my head of Judy crying and then me pushing her down. Even Aunt Bette doesn't believe in pushing each other around in the school yard. Well, it's not like I go around pushing people all the time.

"Did you hear me, Rose? What do you think I should do about Snooty Judy?"

"Um … oh, sorry Sandra. I thought that was great — you asking whether she wanted some of your sandwich. And she just marched away." Again Sandra smiles. Then I add, "My Aunt Bette says, spunk doesn't hang its head."

"I wish Big Hat Bette was *my* aunt."

"You can come with me sometimes when I visit her."

"Oh, you know what Mrs. Gibbons said to me when I asked her why I didn't get into the play?"

"You asked her that?" Sandra's eyes open wide. "I'd *never* be able to do that."

"She said I did well, but sometimes my voice was too high. She said a low voice is stronger than a high voice."

"Umm … but … our preacher says we're supposed to be humble."

"Oh humble-shmumble. There was this spunky Mennonite kid," I tell Sandra, "that I read about in a book Aunt Bette gave me — a girl ten years old in Russia, a long time ago — 1917. Well, there were bandits running around all over the place because there was no government. A mean old bandit came banging on the door in the middle of the night. He wanted the family's money and all their stuff. Well, the family didn't have any money. Except the girl remembered her Christmas coin. She pulled herself up tall, looked the bandit straight in the eye, and said, 'Here, take my Christmas money.' But the bandit got red in the face, kinda shuffled around, then kissed the girl on the cheek, and left, without taking the money or any of the other stuff. Anyway, how humble is that, standing tall in front of the bandit and saving their family's stuff?"

"Humble shmumble," says Sandra. We both laugh and laugh.

"I couldn't have done that!" says Sandra. "Stand up to a bandit like that."

"Maybe you could have."

"Well, he couldn't have been *all* mean, or he would have taken the family's stuff and the girl's coin."

I think about this, then say, "What if Judy isn't mean? I mean down deep — re-e-e-e-al deep."

Sandra's eyes are wide. "Sure has to be awfully deep." She thinks a while, then says, "Nope. She's mean." She points to one of trees on the painting and says in a nasty Judy voice, "That looks like a horse's butt to me."

Again we laugh, but I don't feel as giggly as I did before.

Uh-oh! Mr. Ford. "You two are supposed to be working on the backdrop — doesn't look like you're any farther along than you were when you came in." He talks in a stern voice, but he doesn't look angry at all. Sandra looks up at him in amazement. "That's the first time I've been scolded by a teacher," she says after Mr. Ford leaves. But she looks pleased, like she just got into some special club or something.

\*\*\*

The next Sunday, Sandra and I visit Aunt Bette at her house after church.

"Has the preacher seen that?" Sandra points to a naked sculpture, her eyes wide.

"Well darlin', I don't make a point of showing him, but neither do I hide it. I imagine he's seen it alright, though he hasn't said anything. Maybe he thinks I'm a lost 'cause. The sculpture is called 'The Thinker,' by Auguste Rodin."

The Thinker sits sort of hunched, with his head resting on his fist. Maybe he is thinking about the why of things like I do when I'm with Grandmother Oak. "He's probably thinking important thoughts," I say.

"Maybe," says Sandra, "but does he have to do it *naked*?"

She stares at the floor, her face red. In a quiet voice she says, "My mamma would say the naked sculpture is sin."

"Oh, darlin', come here," says Aunt Bette. "I think I have something you might like better." She puts her arm around Sandra's shoulder and leads her to a sunflower painting. I love sunflowers — the way they turn their big, bright faces towards the sun. "The artist is Claude Monet," says Aunt Bette. "The painting is of Monet's garden."

"I make outdoor scenes, too," says Sandra.

"Gardens and fields and stuff."

"Well, good for you. You and Monet have something in common." The worry on Sandra's face turns into a small smile. "Rose tells me you are an artist," says Aunt Bette.

"An *artist*?" Sandra's mouth drops open. "Oh no! I'm not *that* good."

"From what Rose tells me about your work on the backdrop for your play, I have no doubt at all that you're an artist."

Sandra's small smile turns into a big, beaming sunflower smile. Then she says more seriously, "But I don't do *naked* art."

"You do whatever kind of art is right for you."

I look closely at Monet's garden. Behind the sunflowers is a house, with a path leading through the flowers. A girl is walking down the path and out of the shadows. Oh! Farther back, there is another girl. I didn't even see her at first. But I think she's coming out of the shadows, too. I wonder if there are more children inside the house. I imagine a whole house full of kids, waiting to come out.

# 19

## The Play

"Mamma, please, please, please? I really want to go see *Anne of Green Gables*. Sandra and I worked so hard on the backdrop."

"Pwease, pwease, pwease?" says Daniel.

"We have enough to deal with in real life without getting involved with imaginary happenings in some silly play. No play!" She turns away.

I can't believe it. I stomp from the kitchen to the living room. I just flop down into a chair. But the door is open the tiniest crack, and after a minute I begin to hear mumblings. I go to the door. Can't make out any words. Then Papa's voice gets louder. "Don't do to Rose what your Papa did to you." I hear shuffling, and even … a sob? The footsteps gets nearer, and I get away from the door. Don't want to be caught listening. Then it gets quiet.

I walk casually into the room where they'd been talking, as if I hadn't heard a thing.

Mamma's voice is gruff. "Well, what are you waiting for? Hurry to do your chores, or we'll be late to see your play."

"Oh thank you, Mamma." Without even thinking, I hug her. But her body is all stiff.

I dash to gather the eggs. The same cross old hen sits in the same nest. No time to hold her head down with a stick. I reach under her for the eggs. Peck! Peck! Peck! *Ouch!*

Then I run to help Papa milk. *Zum-zum! Zum-zum!*

***

At last we're all squeezed into our rickety red pickup. It clatters out a rhythm that seems to say, "We're GOING to SEE a PLAY. We're GOING to SEE a PLAY." I chant along with the pickup's

121

rhythm. Daniel laughs and repeats, "We're GOING to SEE a PWAY."

Just before we get there, Papa turns to Daniel and me and says, "You should have heard your Mamma read — poems and such. She was the best reader in our class." Mamma and Papa went to the same school.

"Mamma," I say, "that must be one of your talents too numerous to mention."

"What's numero-dementia?" asks Daniel. Everyone ignores him.

"Mamma, *please* read to us sometimes."

\*\*\*

When we walk into the school building, I feel … yeah … still smurt. The kids in the play are whispering in a buzzy, excited way. And I'm not part of it. We sit down near the front and I try to cheer myself up. Take a good long look at the backdrop. It looks really good. Guess I *am* part of it. Sandra is sitting a few chairs away. I smile at her and point to the backdrop. She beams.

The play begins.

When Cindy, Anne I mean, bashes Tom, ah … Gilbert Blythe, over the head, Daniel gasps. "You're in troub-o now," he calls in a clear, high voice. A big roaring laugh from the audience. Daniel kinda curls into me, embarrassed.

Cindy waits for the laughing to stop, then she holds her head with both hands and repeats, "I'm in trouble now." Again, roaring laughter.

"I tode you," says Daniel, quietly this time.

I gotta admit, Cindy is good. I'll tell her, after the play.

Even Judy does pretty well, playing the part of nosey, know-it-all Mrs. Lynde. Well, she sure has had enough practice being nasty. I keep peeking at Mamma during the play. Mostly she sits kinda stiff with her mouth in a straight line. I look at her during the part about Marilla not wanting Anne to go to a literary evening. Same straight mouth. But a few times she has a tiny smile — like when Anne wears a crown of wildflowers to church. She even leans over and whispers to me, "Reminds me of your Aunt Bette when she was little."

***

After the play, there are lots of people all around Cindy, telling her how good she did. There are so many people that I can't even get to her. Then I see Judy — not so many people around her. Her grumpy-looking papa is here, too — talking to a group of men, and ignoring Judy. He probably doesn't even tell her she did good. Judy is standing beside a thin woman, probably her mamma. The woman is wearing a yellow, flowered dress. Faded, but still kinda fancy — like it used to be real nice. Judy is in a red dress and she looks nicer than I've seen her before. Her cheeks are rosy. I even think about my camp photo. Well she doesn't look *that* nice. Oops, a proud thought. Anyway, it's the first time I've seen her in a dress. Hmmm, should I go to her? Nah! But a whole new person probably would. My spunky feet march over, before my head can argue. "Judy, you did real good," I say.

Judy's eyes fly open wide. She looks down — doesn't even look snobby or anything. "Thanks," she mumbles. She shuffles about, pulls at her mamma's hand and says, "Let's go."

"Just a minute," says the woman. The woman looks at me with dark, piercing eyes. Smiles a little. "Judy tells me you are Mennonite."

"Yes."

"Well, I respect your people a great deal. We've had some good business dealings with Mennonites, buying seeds for planting crops, and such."

Judy's papa comes over. "Come on woman, let's get outa here." His voice is loud.

Judy stares at the floor, and her mamma's face turns red. But she lifts her head, smiles at me and says, "I'm glad you're Judy's friend."

"Bye," I say.

*Judy's friend?* Her mamma thinks I'm her *friend.* Maybe because I came over and told her she did good.

I go over to Cindy. She *does* remind me of my camp photo — all glowy. "You made a real good Anne."

She smiles. "You would have been good, too."

I'm so surprised, tears spring to my eyes.

"Yeah, I *know* you would've been good" she says, "because when I heard you ..." She blushes and puts her hands in front of her mouth.

"What were you gonna say?"

"Um ... well ... I was going past when you were trying out, 'cause I had to go to the washroom, and I heard you yelling all that stuff. You were so good that I listened for a while. I was worried you'd get the part." Again she blushes. "Are you mad? That I listened, I mean."

"Nah."

"You surprised me. I mean you hardly ever talk in class or anything. You sure did yell at that nosey old Mrs. Lynde."

"So did you, tonight, I mean." We both laugh nervous little laughs. We've never talked to each other this much before. "And I loved it how you knew just what to say after my brother called out about you being in trouble."

Cindy smiles the glowiest smile *ever.* "That's called ad libbing, Mrs Gibbons says, when you say something that's not in the script."

And you sure did give Tom — I mean Gilbert Blythe — a good whack over the head."

"Yeah. Catholics aren't supposed to do that."

"Are you *Catholic*?"

"Yeah! And we have rules, rules, rules."

"You too?" I'm amazed. "But you probably don't have as many rules as Mennonites."

"You'd be surprised," Cindy laughs. Then she sees her mamma, turns, and runs into her open arms.

I go to Sandra — put my arm around her shoulder. She looks surprised. We walk to the backdrop. I peer at one of the trees. "Only a great artist could make a horse's butt as good as that," I say. Sandra laughs the biggest laugh I've ever heard her laugh.

# 20

# Catching Heck

Whoop-de-do and hallelujah! Cindy and I are getting to be friends. But I have a tiny worry about this because I'm Sandra's friend, too. And Cindy and Sandra aren't really friends, so it feels sort of funny if all three of us are together. Anyway, other things are happening too. Things feel sort of speeded up in my life. Maybe that's what happens when a person gets spunky all of a sudden. For one thing, Judy isn't the biggest thought in my head anymore. But the best thing is that Cindy and I are practising softball together, though sometimes it's so cold we freeze our fingers. We haven't yet started playing softball in school — any day now.

Today, Cindy and I stay after school to practise ball, though I know I might catch heck for getting home late. Sometimes heck is worth it. I *gotta* be ready for softball this spring. I *gotta, gotta, gotta*! Cindy and I play catch. And pitch for each other while the other hits.

"You're getting so good," she says.

"Sure better than I was."

"My fingers are freezing right off," grumbles Cindy after a while.

"Yeah, mine too."

"Let's go sit against the schoolhouse for a coupla minutes, to get warmer."

We huddle together, pulling our coats around tight.

"Sure wish the school wasn't locked," says Cindy.

I get up and turn the knob, not expecting it to open, but *wonder of wonders*, it opens. We look at each other, amazed. There are no cars around or anything.

"What if there's a burglar in there or something?" I say. "Maybe someone picked the lock."

Eyes wide, we go in anyway. Slowly. We try some of the classroom doors — all locked. We get to our classroom. It's not locked. But no one is in the room. Creepy.

Anyway, it's warm. I sit at my desk, rub my hands together, slap my hands on my desk. "It helps warm my hands," I tell Cindy. I whack the desk harder and think about my first day at Lone Tree. And all of a sudden I decide to tell Cindy. "On my first day of school at Lone Tree, I couldn't stand sitting quietly, so I got out of my desk and ran around the schoolroom banging each desk."

"You did *that?*"

"Yup!"

She giggles.

Before I know it, I start walking around the room smacking each desk, just lightly. Cindy follows. Then I smack a bit harder. Cindy does to. I walk faster. So does she. We go faster, faster, until we're running and whacking — hard! And laughing. I know we're acting like little kids, but *so what*? Finally we plunk to the floor in a giggle fit. And oh, I have to go pee. And we're both howling. "This … is … such *Dummheit*," I shout between groans of laughter.

"Such *Dumm* what?" asks Cindy.

"It means … it means …"

"*What is going on!*" a voice thunders. We both jump up from the floor scared to death. Uh-oh! Mr. Ford.

First a shocked quietness.

"Well?"

"It was cold … and … we were practising ball."

Cindy and I interrupt each other trying to explain. And all the while, I'm in agony. I have to go pee *so bad!*

"And that's why you were running around the classroom like three year olds?"

All the while I'm shuffling from one foot to the other, trying desperately not to pee my pants.

"And what's this dance you're doing?" asks Mr. Ford.

"I have to go to the washroom," I say in a small voice. Now probably isn't the time to use my strong, whole-new-person voice.

"Well go, and then get out of here. I don't even *want* to know what was going on in this room." His voice sounds suddenly tired. "And ..." his voice gets real stern, "I *never* want to see you in the school building after hours without permission *again*."

"No, Mr. Ford," we both say in tiny voices.

Mr. Ford goes to his desk, and I see a pile of our workbooks that we handed in today.

Back outside, we see Mr. Ford's car behind a clump of trees.

"Did he have to hide his car?" asks Cindy. We laugh. I link my arm through Cindy's like I've seen other girls do. It just popped into my head and I did it, but ... what if she doesn't like it? I look at her, feeling a little afraid. But she smiles. *Whoop-de-do!* I've never had an arm-linking friend before.

Yeah, sometimes heck is worth it. I go home to face mine for being late. Two hecks in one day — teacher heck and Mamma heck.

# 21

## Eeny Meeny Miney Mo

Today is the day — the first day since last fall that we're out to play softball. I've got a bad case of the jittery-twitters, even though I play much better than I used to.

What if I strike out like I did so often in the fall?

What if I fumble?

*What if … oh be quiet*, I say inside my head to that what-if voice.

"We'll choose sides," says Tom.

My belly tightens, almost the same as it did last fall. Most kids don't know I've been practising, except for Cindy. Maybe I'll still be chosen almost last. Suddenly I have an idea, so I won't be chosen near the last.

"I'll be one of the choosers," I say before I can change my mind.

"*I'm* choosing," says Judy. But she doesn't say it in a nasty voice. Instead, she sounds worried.

I look her in the eye. "We can both be choosers."

"What?" shouts Tom. He has a look on his face which says: that's the dumbest thing I ever heard.

"Rose and Judy can choose," says Cindy. She smiles at me.

"Hey!" shouts Tom. In the fall, he usually chose.

I stare at him. "You chose lots of times, Tom. I've never had a turn to choose." My voice is calm, but my heart is thumpity-bumping.

"Why should you? You're not good at softball."

I don't answer. Just hold my head high, still looking him in the eye. Cindy and Tom glare at each other. Finally Tom hurls his glove to the ground and stomps to the edge of the group. My heart is still hammering and I feel shaky. This whole-new-person business is *hard work*.

Judy chooses first without asking anyone. She just chooses.

"Tom," she says, looking a little smug. He perks up from his corner and comes to her, grinning. They are the two best players, so maybe their team will win. Doesn't matter. I feel like I won something already.

"Cindy," I say.

"Dennis," says Judy.

My turn. But suddenly I don't feel like choosing after all. What am I going to do about Sandra, who is the worst player? I don't want to choose her last.

"Come *on*," says Tom.

I don't know what to do. Should I choose Sandra?

"What're ya waitin' for?" says Judy.

I kick my toe into the dirt, still not choosing.

"Choosing sides is *stupid!*" I say.

"*You're* the one that wanted to choose," says Tom. *It's true. I asked to choose. How am I going to get out of this muddle?*

Now Dennis is getting twitchy. "Our whole recess will be over before we even get started," he says.

Oh! An idea is hatching in my head. I take a deep breath.

"*Eeny* ..." I point to a kid.

"*Meeny* ..." I point to the next kid in a line of kids.

"She's crazy," someone shouts. Others giggle.

"*Miney* ..." The next kid.

"I knew we shouldn't let her choose," moans Tom.

"*Mo* ..." A big poke towards the next kid.

I make something up quickly, pointing to one kid for each word. "Who's — on — my — team — do — you — know. Y — O — U spells *YOU.*"

The last word lands on Fred. "Fred," I call.

Tom still grumbles. "You *can't* choose *that* way."

"I'm the chooser, and that's the way I choose."

"Well, I'm choosing the normal way."

"And I'm choosing the *eeny-meeny* way."

I'm feeling so good, that when our team goes to the outfield I shout, "I'm shortstop." I've dreamed of being shortstop forever.

As I go to the shortstop spot, I do have worries flurrying in my head.

What if — *stop*, I say to myself.

The first batter strikes out. The second batter hits a grounder to first base. The first baseman scoops it up and the runner is out. The third batter hits a fly ball which — oh my — is coming towards me ... sort of. But it's too far right. I run like mad. *Can I do it?* I make a huge jump and re-e-e-each! *I catch it.* With one hand!

*I did it! I did it! I did it!* Even without a glove.

A tingly, buzzy sting on my hand. Fact is, I buzz and tingle from my toes right to the top of my head. *Whoop-de-do and hallelujah*! I've waited forever to make a catch like this. I'm in such a blurry, happy place inside my head that I don't even know too much about what's happening around me. But I do know Cindy puts her arms around me for just a second. "Hey-ya, Rose." And I see Judy stare, then look away.

After recess, Cindy links her arm into mine when we walk into the school, and I notice two things. Sandra gets a hurt look in her eyes. *I don't like hurting her feelings.* And something about Judy's expression too — hers is harder to figure out. I think it's a sort of a wishing-wanting look. Does she want to be friends? Deep down, I mean.

In the washroom I catch a glimpse of myself in the mirror. My face looks sort of like my camp photo, except that my hair sticks out in every direction, like a jumped-in haystack. I go into the classroom, not even worrying about my haystack-hair.

Tom whispers,

*Eeny meeny miney mo,*
*Rose is crazy, don't you know.*

But he doesn't seem snobby or anything. I smile at him. "Eccentric," I whisper back.

# 22

## Each Minute a Piece of Forever

Hello Grandmother Oak! Hello world! Hello whole new person! I smile, thinking of my flying catch yesterday. Right this minute I feel so-o-o good. I'm so glad spring is here — well almost! It's still cool. I pull my jacket around me. But really soon, warm winds will blow and prairie flowers will bloom all over the place. I especially like the pink wild roses that sprawl, growing as they please, all higgledy-piggledy along the road-side. Grandmother's leaves are still tiny, so I can see lots of sky — so-o-o blue. Fluffy cloud pictures float by — a fat Santa Claus, a butterfly, a tractor with puffs of smoke. I squint. Wisps of blue and white. Oh, an angel cloud! I close my eyes. Sigh. I let my thoughts float with the clouds. Hear a whisper. Each minute is a piece of forever. Was that the angel? Or Grandmother? Or my own thought? Doesn't matter. *Each minute a piece of forever.* Sounds like the start of a poem. I'll work on it sometime. I peek. The angel is still there, but one of her wings is slipping. I close my eyes again. I think about nothing at all.

Drift …

\*\*\*

Don't know if I was asleep or what, but all at once it's sort of like I wake up. It almost feels like I've been away for a while. And there is a whole new picture in the sky. But I haven't yet figured out what it is.

I take a deep breath.

I think about school stuff. Sandra and Cindy — how I'm friends with them both but they're not friends with each other. Do I have to be with them one at a time? Or could I help them be friends? Or what? Anyway, I guess now that I'm sort of spunky, I'll figure it out. And Judy is still in my head, but in a new way. I wonder if something is wrong at her house. Makes me sad to think that.

I think about maybes.

Maybe I'll be in a school play next year.

Maybe I'll even become friends with Judy.

Maybe I'll have lots of friends at camp this summer. Yeah, I'm going again. Mamma wants me to, and I didn't even argue. I wanna go, sort of. I'm only a *little* nervous.

Maybe …

"Rose! Rose!" Daniel is peering into the tree.

I climb down. "Wanna look at pictures in the clouds?" I ask.

We lie on our backs in a patch of green. The ground feels firm on my back — holding me.

"Wook Rose, a rabbit." Daniel points to a puffy cloud bunny with big, long ears.

"Uh-oh! Part of his ear is floating off. Poor rabbit."

Daniel laughs.

The other ear gets short and squishy. Now it's a cat.

Mamma calls, "I need help in the garden. Where *are* you, Rose?" Some things don't change.

"Gotta go, Daniel."

But lots of things do change. I go to Mamma and give her a hug — for no reason except that I feel like it. And wonder of wonders, she hugs me back.

### Grandmother Oak

Cradled in the arms
Of the oak
Breeze strumming
Leaves humming
Lullabies
I rest and dream
Stay still till it seems
My body becomes the trunk
My arms become the branches
My hair becomes the leaves
And my breath becomes the wind

# Author Note

Parts of this story are based on my childhood memories, while others are pure fiction. Like Rose, I grew up Mennonite. I struggled to be accepted, and sometimes felt misunderstood because I was quiet. And I always wondered about the "why of things."

I also had to face schoolyard bullies. Sometimes it was really hard. Mennonites believe that it is important to solve problems in peaceful ways, that fights only 'cause more fights, just like war only causes more wars. So what was I supposed to do when someone picked on me?

Something else I remember from childhood is that some of the adults around me thought many fun things were *Dummheit*. It's a German word that means silliness or even stupidity. These people had firm ideas about how people should live.

Few Mennonites are as strict as in earlier times, though some still live by lots of rules, avoiding modern things and dressing plainly. Lifestyles vary among Mennonites, but most are just ordinary people. And though some early Mennonites stayed apart from the rest of the world, today many are right smack in the middle of things, believing it is best to work where there is a need. For example, Mennonites have worked with other groups to form an organization called Christian Peacemaker Teams. It sends trained peacemakers to troubled and war-torn places all over the world. Others work in peace-building projects, such as those run by the Mennonite Central Committee (MCC). I worked with MCC as a children's daycamp leader in Chicago's inner city.

I still believe in solving problems nonviolently. And I still struggle with how this can be done, because it isn't easy, of course. Yet, I feel that a peaceful solution is the only kind that lasts.

To learn about Mennonites and their beliefs, you can visit the following website: www.thirdway.com/menno.

*— Laurel Dee Gugler*